# THE MAN WHO DIDN'T KNOW TO LOVE

## LOVE TRIUMPHED

## MANUEL TOVAR

# CHAPTER ONE

Now that I have a moment of peace and reflection, I analyze what my life was like in the years of my precocious and crazy adolescence and youth; I was very young but I already wanted to have access to the things that were allowed to older people and with defined criteria, it is not a lack of modesty because one of my few qualities was always telling the truth, although it generally caused me problems of different nature, but the reason for my clarification is to tell the reason for my precocity: at fourteen years of age I already had an inclination towards promiscuity and due to my height and physical strength combined with my good-looking face I was very desired by the sex workers, who although that was their way of livelihood, did not hesitate to offer me their attributes for free.

That was one of the reasons for my addiction to sex, because there was not a day when I did not have the opportunity for action, so as the saying goes "practice makes perfect" and I became the perfect lover (modesty aside). Although I did not miss the opportunity to also be very diligent at school, it turns out that my parents, upset by my actions, made it a condition for me to change my behavior or move somewhere else, since I was being a bad example for my younger sisters and brother. that I.

By good or bad luck, one of the women with whom I had (secret) relationships offered me her support so that I could live in her house; She was a widow with two small children (four and six years old), in addition to being very beautiful, also very beautiful and hard-working. She was a primary school teacher, so she helped me improve my studies, since with her knowledge and her dedication to teaching me she made me a very outstanding student. Although she was twice my age, she was not old, because with her thirty years and the lusciousness of her skin, plus the attributes of her statuesque body, she looked at least twenty or twenty-two years old. We lived in a beautiful place called Ceiba, on the shore of the Caribbean Sea (Honduras) and where we were very happy, although I did not work I made an effort to go fishing every day so that there would at least be a good portion of fish for each one. , it turns out that: when I turned eighteen and after having graduated from high school, I realized that the chances of finding a good job or having the opportunity to attend university were very slim and it was then that I began to mature the idea to emigrate to the USA

By then my benefactor was already thirty-four years old and her children had already grown up and we constantly had scenes of jealousy when seeing that their mother was paying attention to me, so I was a little disappointed in the relationship, so I started dating. whether it was to the park or the square to interact with people of the same age, and accidentally

I met a beautiful girl of approximately seventeen years of age and with whom we got along wonderfully, beginning a friendly relationship but which became something more than that over time. She was a little woman about five ten tall, with wide hips and bulging buttocks, shapely legs and a narrow waist, long and wavy black hair, the perfect oval of her face was decorated by beautiful green eyes, with long, curved eyelashes, her little upturned nose and a striking little mouth with thick and sensual lips that was decorated with two rows of beautiful pearls (for teeth) from her little ears hung some little earrings that gave it the final touch, and then when you looked down you would find one with beautiful and massive breasts that made you morbid when thinking about her body with skin tanned by the tropical sun. Her name was Dalila, always radiant with joy and with her suggestive and flirtatious look that made any man turn to look at her, even if he later ignored them with the whip of indifference.

Well, when I turned eighteen my body had undergone some changes, I was taller (about six feet) and more athletic, my skin was white but tanned, my hair wavy and brown, my eyes blue and my features very manly, bearded and hair on his chest and a rather European profile (since my mother had been the product of a French sailor and my native grandmother). I had gotten a job at one of the town's gas stations but I couldn't get used to the idea of wasting my time there, so while talking to Dalila I told her about my concerns that didn't differ much from hers, as fate would have it one afternoon. We were able to contain our animal impulses and we fell into one of the greatest experiences. When I made it my own, I discovered that I was the first man in his sexual awakening. It was something wonderful because I had always been with women with extensive experience, so that situation she sublimated me in such a way that I felt morally obliged to repair her dignity as a woman, I suggested that the next day I would go ask for her hand but she did not accept, on the contrary, she asked me that we take our time and that there would be an opportunity to do so. something about.

And a relationship began in which our hunger for the pleasure of having each other did not leave us still, because as soon as it got dark we headed to the place where we forgot that anyone other than us existed, we got involved in an intense and frenetic body to body, where the energy of our youth combined with our growing love, filled our surroundings with energy, forming a field that mystified our union. It had become a vice or something similar, because I was not happy if I did not have the opportunity to be by her side, even if it was only to drink the nectar from her delicious mouth, to caress her delicate skin or squeeze her beautiful, solid breasts, to slide my hands through her fragrant hair, which slowly descended until they gently rested on her bulging buttocks.

It was unsettling when I wasn't by her side, so sexual relations with my benefactor named Rosaura had fallen into a tense and monotonous impasse, so making a great effort I started a clarifying conversation with such a good person. That night and after the children had gone to bed, my clarification began: I want you to let me speak and analyze well all the things that I am going to explain: first; I want you to understand that although I love you, perhaps it is an affection of gratitude and that is not love, second; I thank you infinitely for the opportunity you have given me to share with me all your academic knowledge so that I could move forward in my studies, at the same time that you gave me shelter and food when I needed it most and did not hesitate to give me your love and your body to satisfy my instincts without thinking about the consequences, in addition to instilling in me good customs and religious principles. I know that here I don't have many chances of getting ahead, so I have decided to go to the United States where at least there is a lot of work... he didn't let me continue, he began to sob bitterly, he took me by the hands and pleadingly told me: no. Go away André, please, I begged you, you know that would cause me death, you know how much I love you... please don't be cruel... tell me what you want me to do, because for you I am capable of anything, even giving my life if I do. you ask.

I couldn't bear Rosaura's suffering, but I had to be energetic and after drying her tears I promised her that I wouldn't forget her and that as soon as I was in a good financial situation I would send for her. I kissed her and felt her warm body between me. I could not forget so many nights of lust and dalliance in my arms and we fell into a passionate night of pleasure, of maddening kisses, of intense caresses and electrifying orgasms that had a sad taste of farewell, of a goodbye that was causing my soul to tremble for the restlessness of my ungratefulness. The truth is I didn't know if fate would give me the opportunity to see her again, but I had made a promise to help her financially so that her children could also get ahead, in the same way that I graduated thanks to her help.

I got up very early and after taking a revitalizing bath I began to organize my things, a couple of complete changes and a bag for my back (Back pack), she could not hide her sadness and at times she could not contain her crying so She went into the bedroom to sob, her children who were already leaving for school asked her, What's wrong, mom? And she, still with tears in her eyes, managed to say...nothing, go away, you're going to be late.  It broke my heart to see her in a terrible situation, but I had already made my plan and there was no way to change it. I approached to say goodbye, but she composed her attitude and invited me to have breakfast before leaving. While I was at the table, she asked me: Who are you going with? As if he sensed my infidelity and knew of my plans in their entirety, but I cunningly told him that I would go alone. I don't know if she believed my answer or not, but at the end of it all...she said goodbye with a soft and motherly kiss, wishing me luck and giving me her blessing.

Oh destiny, capricious destiny that insists on playing with the lives of men, you who are a cheater and captivate anyone, I ask you for what you want most that you stay away from me and let me play my luck. I wanted it not to be destiny that marked my route, but rather for luck to be in my favor on the long path that I had proposed, so I passed by the place where Dalila would supposedly be waiting for me and who, after seeing me, headed to my meeting to go to the bus stop. I asked Dalila to sit a few rows back, because I had the feeling that Rosaura might show up to make sure if I was really traveling alone, although it didn't matter much anymore, at least I wanted her to be less hurt in her feelings, because I considered that he didn't deserve it.

And my forebodings had some truth, because a few minutes before the bus left for the border with Guatemala, Rosaura appeared looking through the windows of the bus and upon seeing me she got into the bus and, addressing me, handed me a scapular and a plastic bag containing some money, I was moved but I couldn't do anything other than thank him, he took my hands again and asked me to take care of myself and to write to him as soon as I arrived, which I ceremoniously promised him. She got off and waited for the bus to leave. I still remember her eyes full of tears and her little hand saying goodbye, showing a grimace of helplessness and despair on her face. It broke my soul, it moved my most intimate feelings, I also felt like crying, getting off the bus and asking him to forgive me for the harm I was causing him, for the pain I was causing such a kind soul, but there was no longer any. remedy the damage had already been done and only time, the counselor time would make him heal the wounds that I had caused him. And may God forgive me for what I was making her suffer.

The bus began its journey, took a turn along the central street and passed near the beach, it let us see for the last time the green and strong palm trees that swayed to the rhythm of the wind of the high tide, we could see once again the white sands of the beach that were stirred by the effect of the waves that caressed them, it was a melancholic farewell, intriguing because we did not know what awaited us but we trusted it was something very good. And the roar of the engine began to lull us to sleep, to tell us that little by little we were moving away from what had been our home for many years, to get closer to the unknown, to adventure and perhaps to a chain of vicissitudes and hardships, to mature through experience, to become stronger through the blows of life.

We passed through Tela, San Pedro, a fairly large city compared to our birthplace, but just as hot and beautiful but especially still our own country, we continued devouring kilometers and passing towns and villages, Lima, the entrance to the Ruinas, Santa Rosa de Copan, Nueva Ocotepeque and we arrived at Aguas Calientes, the border with Guatemala, although it was Central American territory, it began to be a different country from ours, where we were no longer citizens but began to be immigrants

The bus took us there, then we had to take one to the capital of Guatemala, but I suggested to Dalila that we first visit the Christ of Esquipulas, to ask him to accompany us on our odyssey and that we arrive safely at the place. From our destination, we arrive at the town of Esquipulas and after finding the Temple we head up the stairs that lead to the entrance of the Temple. Although I was not a good devotee, I tried my best to ask for his protection and showed my humility by kneeling before his Image. I believed that he was the intermediary to communicate with the Elder God and I entrusted him with our well-being and our future.

After long minutes of mysticism and prayer, we went out to look for the bus that would take us to the Capital and where we hoped to spend the night, to leave the next morning in the continuity of the trip. Luckily and because we spoke the same language, in addition to having the same behavioral characteristics, we went unnoticed and had no setbacks to start the new journey. After arriving in Guatemala City, and after having stayed in a very familiar little hotel, we decided to take a good bath and when we were both naked under the shower, caressed by the warm water, we couldn't stand the contact of our bodies. falling into a maelstrom of repressed impulses during our trip and urgently we left the bathroom to fall into an encounter that bordered between the wild and the passionate, between the romantic and the sublime and that's how we stayed until fatigue took over our bodies and forced us to surrender to the presence of Morpheus, after having had an unforgettable night.

Although we had fallen asleep due to fatigue, it seemed as if the stress or anxiety of the trip gave us vitamins to recover quickly and we decided that since we had the opportunity, it would be good to spend a day in the Capital to have the opportunity to see something of That country is so beautiful and full of history, so we moved to different places of which the hotelier had references. We went to the Hipódromo del Norte, the Sauce and the Zapote, the Obelisco and the Aurora (Zoo of La Capital) where we had the opportunity to eat some Chapines snacks such as: atol de elote, chuchitos, tostadas with sauce and chiles stuffed in pirujo bread . We strolled through the little streets of the zoo, entertained by the great variety of wild animals, birds and reptiles as well as some games that are the attraction of the park. As night began to fall we headed back to the little hotel to rest a little from the long walk. and to enjoy our privacy just like the night before. There were no parameters for our love, we had no stipulated time, what we had was irrepressible desires to fulfill each other and given our youth, our love and our fieryness it always seemed that time was not enough and we gave in only to fatigue. ...which was our worst enemy.

Lying in bed, fainted after the exhausting delivery, we stared at the ceiling of the room and as if we sensed something that only our instincts were telling us, we agreed on the question that left our lips in unison... don't you think that Would it be good to work a little here, and then continue with more resources? It seemed as if we were afraid to move forward, but trusting in good luck I told him: don't worry, with what we have, we arrived at the Tijuana border, so you better go to sleep and rest because after a while we will need the strength.

And dawn came and we left with hope in our hearts, with the conviction of our purpose and confidence in our strength and youth to move forward with our effort and work. We headed to eighteenth street at the train station to take the bus, on ninth avenue and where we ate something in a small restaurant before boarding to Ciudad Tecún Umán, where after crossing the Suchiate River we would enter the territory. Mexican. It seemed that the drivers were having a car competition, because as soon as they left a toll booth they began their crazy race that made one entrust their soul to all the saints ever and ever, however it was still exciting because they made use of his professional ability.

And the different towns that were left on the way to the border, Villa Nueva, Amatitlán, began to parade one by one. Precisely as we were passing in front of this last place we were able to see towards the right side of the bus the imposing figure of the Majestic Volcano of

Agua, giant and mute witness of so much history and devastating events that took place in the Capital of the Ancient City of Guatemala. It was an imposing volcano with its wide slopes full of vegetation, with its peak eroded by different eruptions and mischievous clouds that caressed its crater, as if wanting to remove the appearance of a spitter of water and mud.

We continued our journey excited by the skill of the pilot who boasted of his vast experience, we had lost our fear when we realized that he knew what he was doing but that did not take me away from the fear I felt in the face of the unknown, because although he had the appearance of a man strong in my subconscious were still the fears of childhood.

We continued passing through different towns, Palín, Escuintla, Santa Lucia, Cocales, San Antonio and as we approached Mazatenango suddenly and after making a change of speed the bus began to lose its power of movement, so the pilot began to try to find a place where he could check what the problem was and it was after having entered said city where he found the appropriate place. We are very sorry, ladies and gentlemen, but the bus will not be able to continue to its final destination, the transmission broke and we will have to take it to the workshop. The next bus will come in about an hour and you will all transfer to it. It was then that I commented to Dalila that there were already many coincidences, as if something was warning us to change our plans and take our time, which at the end of the day was what we had the most, she suggested that we ask for the value of the ticket and We would spend the night there that night and put some alternative plan into perspective.

Luckily we found a motel in front of the Bus Terminal and after registering we went for a walk along one of the avenues of the City, this avenue took us directly to the Central Park full of flowers and some trees of various sizes, but it was one especially the one that caught our attention, it was a tree that, according to a sign, was on the fence that protected it; It was one hundred and twenty years old, tall, leafy and the most curious thing was that its beautiful and fragrant flowers came out of the same trunk giving it its special touch. It was a hot but humid tropical climate, so we ate something very light and headed to the hotel with morbidity already running through our restless minds.

It would be another night of frenetic kissing, tireless flirting, and electrifying, non-stop orgasms that were the culmination of our young love. After we were all lying on the bed fainted and still breathing heavily, I asked Dalila: do you think it would be a good place to take a break in our trip? He replied: let's do an inspection in the morning and then we will look at the possibilities and then we will talk, it seemed very reasonable to me and after accepting the idea we fell asleep with our hands clasped.

We got up early and after doing a short tour we realized that it was a small city and that most of the businesses were operated by the same owners, so after eating some fruits of good quality and exquisite flavor we tackled the next bus that was going towards our destination. I still remember the pilot's assistant loudly announcing the final destination of the route, announcing as if in recital all the intermediate points that would be passed. And we started the trip again hoping that this time there would be no incident that would hinder the trip.

We passed the town of Cuyotenango, Palmares and other small towns until we reached Coatepeque where we made a fifteen-minute stop. We felt that we were very close to reaching the border and that predisposed us to anxiety and nervousness, so we tried to Ignoring them, we insist on trying to keep in our memory the highlights of such a laborious place. All the people on the street looked like wind-up dolls, they walked as if someone was chasing them and they bought and sold and never sat still, their tenacity was admirable. And the fifteen minutes were up and we started the journey again, this time we knew that there was very little left because we had asked one of the passengers and he confirmed the time it would be to the coveted border.

We arrived around five in the afternoon and thinking that we did not know the place we decided to go the next day, thinking that it would be better to do it in daylight so as not to have problems with the currents when crossing the river. We looked again for a place to spend the night, it was a small hotel of very humble condition but that radiated cleanliness and kindness on the part of the owners, a couple in their fifties who, trying to be friendly, offered to tell us where the crossing was easiest. since the river was wider but less deep. So after talking for a while with them and eating some tasty snacks at the same time, we decided to go to sleep, trying to mitigate the feeling of fear that was affecting us and perhaps to have a moment of pleasure to preserve the memory. of our last night in Bella Guatemala.

And dawn came... and after taking a tasty bath with cold water we had a light breakfast, and after saying goodbye to such kind people we began our walk towards the river, which promised to be exciting although not difficult since we were good swimmers. As soon as we arrived at its bank we were surprised to see the crowd crossing in different ways, some perched on different kinds of improvised transportation and for which they charged a price depending on which one was supposedly the safest. We didn't want to go through there, not because we didn't pay, but because on the other side of the river there were some police officers and they were probably asking us questions or asking us for papers, (documents) which we had torn up the night before.

We walked down the river according to the reference of the Lords of the Hotel until we found a huge pool that seemed to be less strong in its current, we took off all our clothes until she was only in her bra and underwear and I was only in boxers and after putting the clothes in a plastic bag we began our crossing to the other side of the river. Everything was so quiet that you could only hear the chirping of some birds and the noise of the stream sliding downhill, but in the overwhelming silence you could feel a strange sensation of fear, of innate restlessness.

# CHAPTER TWO

We were good swimmers because we were born in a port, so crossing the river had not been very difficult despite its strong current, so in a matter of a few minutes we were emerging on the other bank; It was a semi-wooded area with some huge rocks that had probably been washed away by the river floods many years ago and after taking shelter behind the huge rocks we proceeded to take off the few clothes to wring them out and put them on again, they would dry out in the heat. what was he doing. We continued to feel that fear of something unknown, something that our subconscious tried to warn us about but that we couldn't decipher, so after putting on my pants and shirt and she put on her shorts and blouse, we started walking along a path that led into between the semi-grove trying to reach the road to get some means of transportation.

We were so engrossed in our appreciation of the green panorama that we did not realize that some individuals were under one of the trees next to the path and where on the other side a mound of large stones was erected, they were as if chatting without realizing our presence. but it was not like that, so sensing danger, I ordered Dalila not to leave me and, trying to be friendly, I greeted them asking them to allow us passage. They responded to the greeting and stood aside, but having already passed, They asked us where are you going? Trying to get us to stop and answer, fools, when we answered again we did not realize that two other guys came out from behind the stones and approaching us threatened us, one with machetes and the other two with knives. , except for the fifth who only bothered to say: do what I'm going to tell you and you won't get hurt. Deliver what you bring of value and we will let you go, Dalila began to tremble in dismay and told me in a low voice; They are going to kill us, let's give them whatever money we have and don't resist because it could be worse.

I was a very determined and strong man, but in the presence of weapons and the number of them that exceeded my expectation of winning, I had to choose to hand over what I had in my pockets and she what she had in a small purse, which was received by the one who acted as the boss, however one of them said: don't think that's all, they surely have something else stuck (hidden, according to the language of the underworld) so the boss this time ordered us to get off. shoes and clothes, I immediately got angry and complained...don't overdo it because the police will find out and they will have problems.

The guy answered: that's what I ask for my alms (I always do it) and he urged us to take off our clothes, which we reluctantly did, she was more embarrassed than me because her beautiful attributes were too noticeable, she instinctively covered her darkest parts.

intimate and I looked embarrassed, the guys, having the clothes, began a thorough inspection, realizing that we were telling the truth because of what the boss said: you can leave and be careful not to yell at us (give them away) and he began to leave, saying let's go, but One of the guys with a depraved face quickly approached the boss and whispering something in his ear, he ordered him to stop. It was then that those with the machetes approached me in a defiant and threatening position with the machetes in hand. The other two stood up. They rushed to take Dalila's hands and, placing the knives a few centimeters from her face, told her: you better cooperate because you wouldn't look very pretty if I caressed you with this knife. She begged and cried and in my desperation I pounced on one of them trying to take the machete from her and be able to defend her from the attack.

I almost managed it, but when I grabbed one of the ruffians by the arm that was holding the machete, the other gave me a cut on the back that stopped me in my attempt, then he gave me a strong blow on the head with the handle of the machete. machete that knocked me to the ground, as I fell to the ground Dalila screamed don't kill him! I'll do whatever you want... and sobbing profusely, they took her behind the stone mound. While I was lying on the ground and with the tip of the machete on my neck, I could only hear the moans of my poor Delilah as she was savagely raped by the first evil born, then it was the next's turn... and the other, when they finished his abominable act the first three one of them came to relieve the one who had me with the machete on my neck from his job while I was bleeding to death, with his vulgar comment he said to him and the other who served as support to the one with the machete: Hurry up, it's very good... I'll take care of the dead man and the other two ran to continue the task, to become birds of prey, to devour the prey that remained on the ground, defenseless, beaten and bleeding, without even the breath to moan. because she was faint, on the verge of unconsciousness.

After their disgusting act they left us for dead, thinking that there was nothing more to do, perhaps thinking that the other birds of prey would take good care of us. They were wrong because although I had lost a considerable amount of blood, I gathered my strength and got up to look for Delilah, I almost crawled to get to her side and when I saw her lying there as if she were dead, I felt a feeling of emptiness in my heart. stomach, a deep wave of heat invaded my face and a thirst for revenge took over my being, I approached the body that was lying inert and took her in my arms, feeling guilty for what had happened to her, thinking that she was dead. Seeing that he reacted, I left his side and ran or as best I could to collect the things that were scattered with the desire to find a small bottle of water that I had in my back bag.

I lifted her off her torso and offered her a few drinks of water, I asked her: How are you feeling? She said: I'm going to live... but my whole body hurts; It was then that I realized that a trickle of blood was running down between his legs and taking off the shirt that had my blood on his back, I tore it to put the half that was somewhat clean in the middle of his legs to mitigate the bleeding he was having. She picked up her clothes that were all trampled on, although I don't know if it was more than her pride and her feminine dignity, or her ego as a respectable woman and the injuries on her body that seemed to be serious.

 After getting dressed, I helped her stand up and, making a great effort, we headed down the same path trying to find a place where they could help us. We walked for an hour or so until we managed to get out on the road. We stopped under the shade of a tree until, by good luck, a pickup truck passed by and its driver, seeing us and seeing that we had blood on our clothes, deigned to stop. What happened to them? And in general terms we told him that we had been assaulted by some ruffians and that we needed to go to a hospital. The man, perhaps forty years old, very moved, took us to the hospital in Tapachula where he left us, but not before giving me his address. and two hundred pesos in addition to lamenting our situation.

When I admitted her to the emergency room, I no longer had the opportunity to be by her side, but I warned her that I would be waiting for her or until it was possible to go in to see her and for her to say that she lived in a village in the south of the state, the same thing that I would do, well, too. I was treated in the same emergency with the difference that after being sutured I was discharged and was only given some antibiotics. It was nightfall and I was neither hungry nor sleepy, I just wanted to find a way to take revenge on the evil born who were capable of doing us so much harm, without thinking that we were also human and that we deserved respect, but I would not stop until I found them and did them. pay for their crimes. That night passed with me sitting on the benches in the hospital emergency room waiting for dawn to find out about Dalila's health. That night tasted like the bitterest night of my life, the saddest memory a man can carry in his life. his mind for his entire existence and that would have relevant effects on the way I act.

The next morning, very early the police arrived to file a report and they called me as a witness to see if I could recognize the criminals, of course I would recognize them even if they were among a million people, because that type of beings do not look alike. nothing to an ordinary person, furthermore my purpose was to find them myself and get paid in a very exemplary way. So they did not consider me a potential witness and simply said that they would continue with the investigation.

Later, when visiting time arrived, I went to see Delilah who covered her face with her hands and tried to look away when talking to me. She felt ashamed and was not able to look me in the eyes. I, on the other hand, felt sorry for her. of the very traumatizing situation to which I had been subjected, but that was not all, even without looking at my face he told me: I suffered severe damage to my internal organs and they had to cut off part of my womb that was seriously damaged, so that I am no longer worth it as a woman, because I will no longer be able to give you children and have a home as we had planned... and I sob uninterruptedly for long minutes, without paying attention to my words of encouragement that came from the bottom of my loving heart. With part of the two hundred pesos I bought him a cupcake and told him: don't worry, these are things that were not planned and for some reason happen, the important thing is that I still love you the same as always and in the United States we have to find a doctor who can reverse that situation and we will fulfill our dreams as we have planned.

While she was in the hospital I had begun to mobilize to see how I could find a job and raise money to continue the trip, or wait for her to fully recover, due to my personal appearance in addition to my high school knowledge, soon. I was rewarded with a job in one of the hotels in the City where I was offered food and lodging for both of us (with Dalila) because I had told the owner and manager of the hotel about our situation. Not all people are selfless in helping and he was no exception, because when he realized our situation he offered to pay me perhaps half of what he paid the former employee (as I later learned from another employee) but nevertheless ways was enough for us given our situation.

She left the hospital and was very happy to see me standing at the exit, although when she spoke to me she did so by directing her gaze elsewhere, she did not stop being happy, even more so when I told her that we had a place to live and food guaranteed while she recovered. complete. We arrived at the hotel and when the owner of the hotel met her, he was impressed by her beauty and beauty and promised that he would also give her a job when she was in good health, although I had not told him about the attack to which she had been subjected. She was on rest for a month, until she got her period and the doctor discharged her, advising her to have a sexual diet for at least one more month. Although sex was part of our life, we tried to spiritualize ourselves more and dedicate ourselves to the deepest love, the one that can withstand any tough challenge, the love that has sex only as a complement.

The day came when after giving her a test on how she made the beds, they gave her the position of waitress and to celebrate I took her to eat tacos at a famous taqueria, then we took a walk through the park, thinking about it while we delighted in a delicious ice cream popsicle. He was already looking at me more directly and the only thing he didn't do was look me straight in the eyes, but despite everything his mood had been changing and he had begun to be happier than the first days after the event. She was my adoration, I felt complete only when I had her close to me, so the days she was in the hospital were constant suffering, but I kept it to myself because I didn't want her to feel guilty that I suffered for her. I wanted her but I was afraid that when I had her the moments in which I heard her moan would come to my mind, I don't know if for pleasure, or pain, or who knows for what reason, so I better put up with faking any situation so as not to possess her.

She cried silently at night when she thought I was asleep, perhaps crying out of helplessness as she felt like a devalued peso, like a car that has been crashed and no longer has appeal for its owner, or like a garment that was stained and She no longer has vanity to use, she cried and I couldn't think of anything to remedy her crying, for which I felt extremely guilty. And so a few days passed, until one night, waiting for her to be inconsolably crying, I gathered my courage and, turning on the nightstand lamp, I faced her, dried her tears, and drawing her towards me, I kissed her on the mouth. I began to kiss her. timidly until when the monster of desire woke up I continued kissing her passionately to the point of delirium, those kisses that became caresses all over her neck, her shoulders, and then descended towards her beautiful breasts that were an enervating agent for my lustful mind, those that made my body burn with morbid desires, desires to possess her to the point of exhaustion, to give her my manly essence in rhythmic movements that would make her also vibrate in unison and release the instincts repressed for reasons that were extremely unpleasant. And the night passed without wanting it to pass, without wanting it to dawn so as not to separate us, wanting to stop time for an eternity so as not to stop loving each other, possessing us in endless orgasmic cycles until Father Cronus ordered otherwise.

But it dawned, our desires were not enough, which at the end of the day were the desires of some poor mortals with a complex of omnipotent beings, it dawned because it was logical, but what was illogical was that insane way of giving ourselves over to the pleasures of Aphrodite, the way so complex to unite our bodies but also our souls that it seemed they were made for each other, that love that in the most difficult moments was capable of uniting us more, of making us stronger in the face of adversity... blessed love.

It was the medicine that she was missing, it was the medicine that they couldn't give her in the hospital, it was the medicine that her anguished soul, her hurt heart and her loving affection towards me needed. It was the missing link in the chain that united our loving hearts, it was the fuel our relationship needed to continue its loving march.

One of those nights I confessed to him that one of my purposes was to go look for those ill-born people to make them pay for the damage they had done to us, to wash away with blood the damage that they might cause to other innocents who crossed their path, Well, I was aware that this type of people do not deserve to live since they are parasites of society and therefore must be removed from circulation. She listened to me attentively and after meditating for a moment she told me: we do not want to occupy the position of our Higher Being, only he has the right to give or take lives and to punish in the most appropriate way, if you kill them you will not only be putting you on the same level as them, but later you will also deserve punishment and you will lose your qualities that have identified you as an exceptional being, the wounds of the body heal and even if it takes a little longer, those of the soul will also heal, so let's heal them with the passage of time and then there will be other things to worry about, ask your Higher Self and let time pass... time erases everything.

A lot of time had passed, and as the situation at the hotel was getting uncomfortable since the boss had fallen in love with Dalila and began to harass her, we decided that the best thing would be to continue the trip, so we thanked the loving boss for the work. and the widespread help he had provided us, we said goodbye and continued our journey. Now we had one more weapon to avoid any setbacks, we learned the names of all the towns in the State as well as the accent when speaking that was very different from ours, in addition to a couple of birth certificates. We went to the bus station and bought a direct ticket to the Federal District of Mexico, it would be a trip of approximately two days and along the way we would think about what the next step would be, which of course had not changed from the final destination which was Los Angeles, California. . The bus started on its way, as if it knew in advance where it was going and the engine started with its monotonous roar that gradually lulled us to sleep, and that transported us to a semi-conscious dream that always kept us in expectation and It let us know that we were together and united hand in hand.

Soon it became dark and, lacking daylight to observe the landscape, we decided to rest with the idea of having enough strength, since we did not know what effort awaited us in the future. The pilots drove all night and only stopped at dawn so that we passengers had the opportunity to have a quick breakfast. After being energized by the delicious food and having continued the trip, we dedicated ourselves to observing the landscape and memorizing every detail. of the beautiful places we passed. Something that was captured in our minds was the magnificent volcano with its snowy tip and which is located near the state of Puebla, which inspired us how big and powerful it can be without harming anyone.

Seeing her out of the corner of her eye with her gaze enthralled in observing the places we were passing, I began to think about the damage that I had unconsciously caused her, because if I had not involved her in my crazy adventure or made her part of a dream, it surely would not have happened to her. absolutely nothing, she would not feel embarrassed and I would not feel frustrated by the unspeakable event.

The bus continued its unbridled race, the hoarse roar of the engine continued mercilessly, announcing to us that it was putting all its effort into helping us reach our destination and we understood the message and continued making castles in the air, momentarily forgetting the bad memories that tormented us. We had become accustomed to the way of speaking of the natives of the Country, that some people who happened to speak to us automatically asked us what State we were from, so we felt very confident in our purpose.

The bus continued devouring miles and as we got closer, the anxiety and uncertainty of what awaited us increased, begging the Higher Being that this time it would be something better than before. To begin with, one of the passengers who identified himself as a good person, told us that when we arrived we should try to leave the bus station as soon as possible, since there were some judicial officers who asked for documents and for large donations, I don't know if it was true but Because of the doubts we were already warned and we would try not to fall into that situation.

In reality we did not have much luggage, just a couple of bags for our backs so it would be easier to leave said terminal. As soon as we arrived and parked the bus we jumped as if propelled by springs that had been prepared to launch us with their momentum and We headed to the exit without thinking about anything other than being as far away as possible, we only slowed down when we were at a considerable distance. We began the tour without a fixed direction, it was something very different from what we had seen until that moment, people everywhere, people talking in unison that made us get a little confused by so much hubbub, then cars and more cars in all directions and like if they were competing against each other. Stores selling all kinds of items and people calling passers-by to arouse their attention and to be able to sell them something, tall buildings and many churches... all very beautiful and intoxicating, but soon the spell of so many new things passed and we returned to our concern of getting the new transportation to travel the next journey that will take us to the blessed northern border.

By pure coincidence we found a beautiful Church, which we entered to calm our souls at the same time as asking for a little help from the one who can do everything. After leaving it we realized that in the atrium there was a champurrado seller. and refried tamales, so we ate and drank and continued walking, but now we had a defined point...and it was the subway station heading to the northern terminal. As we walked a few blocks to reach the station, we saw an imposing Church and it occurred to me to ask a passerby who told me it was the Basilica of Our Lady of Guadalupe, so postponing access to the subway station we headed to the Basilica to get to know it and ask the Virgin to accompany us on our journey.

We were not devotees, but we had faith in the existence of a Higher Being and therefore we felt identified in the Majestic Church, after praying for a few minutes and already well exalted we let ourselves be carried away by curiosity and toured the Beautiful and Holy place, In addition to being a work of art in its architecture, it is also a mystical place because you can feel the Divine presence.

We went out onto the street again, this time we were confident that our journey was going to be completely safe, we knew that our Guardian Angel would go with us until we reached our established destination and that there would be no human power that could against divine designs. Finally we reached the North Terminal and after buying the direct ticket to Tijuana we boarded the bus to continue the trip. We sat waiting for the bus to have its full load of passengers and start moving. We didn't have to wait long because a few minutes later we got going, it was time to start again mentally photographing the most beautiful things that happened along the way, to enjoy the beauties that nature put at our disposal and to continue making plans , that those abounded in our minds.

Every time I looked at her face I could see in her big eyes, apart from sadness, also a spark of hope and joy when imagining the beautiful things that a woman in the age of dreams stores in her mind, who knows...maybe the idea of that everything would be more beautiful, perhaps to have what we had not had in our poor homeland. Now would be the opportunity to put into practice the English that I had studied at school as a second language, now would be when I would take advantage of the hours I spent burning my eyes to learn Shakespeare's Language in the company of Rosaura, I missed her because She was a special woman, she was authoritarian but knew how to order, she was very serious in public life but sublime in the things of love, she knew how to love and be loved, she was very neat and knew how to cook, and she also owed him everything she was now because she He insisted that I learn well.

It was a mix of feelings that at times confused me, but there were also my hopes of progressing in life and using my gratitude to compensate in some way for the sacrifices that Rosaura had made to ignore the criticism of the people, the sacrifices she made. to buy me clothes so that I was decently dressed, in addition to instilling in me good customs and habits of conduct, as well as respect for divine laws.

I had to concentrate on the most basic thing up to that moment and that was to reach our destinations safe and sound, as well as healthy to do any job, no matter how hard it was. During the time I was working at the gas station I had the opportunity to learn to drive all types of motor vehicles, from a small car to a bus or haul truck, so I had one more weapon with which I would try to make a living.

I was still lost in my thoughts that I had paid little attention to the beauty of the Mexican countryside, but at Dalila's request I focused again on observation and we continued in communication regarding the things that stood out most from each panorama that changed every moment in the long distance of the journey.

And although we were entrusted to our Higher Being, there is never a shortage of someone who wants to interfere with his designs and it happened that when we made a stop in Guadalajara, an official from a certain type of official institution approached us and, asking for documents, took us off the bus, I I showed him the birth certificates and with great poise and trying my best accent I told him that we were going to Tijuana to visit a relative, to which he replied ironically: I don't care who you are going to see but if you don't bother (contribute) you will I'm going to deport you, so it's fifty dollars, I'll leave you alone to search your belongings... and he left the little room in which he had introduced us for a couple of minutes. In reality, the fifty dollars we had left him was a big loss, but we would find a way to get it back, at least we had the opportunity to continue on the path.

And there was one more checkpoint missing where we had to leave the happy forced contribution and according to one of the passengers the one at the exit of the Tijuana bus terminal was missing, so our financial resources were getting smaller as we continued to advance. , so I told Dalila that we should carry out the same operation that we did when we arrived in the Federal District. The location of the bus terminal was different from that of the DF  And we all had to go through different doors that had two officials from State institutions and those who asked for documents indiscriminately. We tried to wait for a favorable situation to go unnoticed, we were lucky because when we were having problems with a large family, one of the guards asked for help from the other who left his post unattended for a few minutes, which allowed us to pass like racing cars in search of freedom.

We could never forget the Beautiful Guaymas Sonora and the beautiful Mazatlán, such charming places and those that motivated my promise to visit them the first opportunity we had and that would be a priority when we now have our residence in the United States. But we had to return to reality, we were already in Tijuana and we had to thank those who had asked for their protection to achieve this, so making an obligatory stop and joining our hands we said a quick and deep prayer and asked for wisdom to achieve the new journey, which was perhaps the shortest but the most difficult, given the effectiveness of the Border Patrol in detecting immigrants crossing the border.

Now we had to cut cash and review our financial funds to pay for the crossing of said border, so entering a small restaurant and going to the bathroom I did the math on what we had left. We only had four hundred dollars so I thought: we were going to need to see what we could do to get the rest, so telling Dalila we began to plan a strategy to earn what was needed. She, with the sweetness that characterized her, and after ordering some tacos, approached the young woman who had served us and asking her a few questions as well as some confidences, she got the aforementioned woman to promise to help her. After speaking with the owner of the taqueria, who asked him some questions and also asked if he was actually related to the other employee (which the two had already agreed upon), he gave the job to Dalila.

The young woman named Anna had asked Dalila to stay a little longer so that she could learn about the orders and that she would also do everything possible so that her parents would give us a little place in their house while we found a place to live, it seemed that it helped her. divine was coming through a person who did not know us, but who had still demonstrated his human quality and his compassion for a woman like her.

After finishing her shift and realizing Dalila's dedication to work, we went to her house on public transportation, which we arrived at as night fell. When we met Anna's family we realized the reason for her human quality, it was a very beautiful family, the father Don Juan José and the mother Doña Inés, her two little sisters Teresa and María who were introduced by our hostess to whom We had given him our names beforehand. The mentionable thing about our first impression was the politeness of all the family members, apart from the correct way of dressing of the women, they all wore their dresses below the knee and with necklines that did not give cause for any morbidity. We were satisfied with the way they treated us and the mention they made of their religious faith since they were members of a religious congregation and we agreed on some of our points of view in the definition of our Higher Self.

Anna's father gave the order for the girls to be placed in the same room and for us to live in the other while we managed financially and in the meantime he told me: that the girls were preparing for their end-of-year exams in first and second year. secondary school degree (Junior High School) so I offered my help since (forgive my modesty) I had been an outstanding student; which he appreciated and I promised that every afternoon and after working on whatever was possible, I would teach them everything they needed to know.

It was time to sleep and after having a small snack we said goodbye, to get a good night's sleep because we already needed it. It dawned and we got up very early in the morning, it was something common for us and after Dalila helped in the kitchen, we had breakfast and after that I said goodbye to go out to look for a job so that our path would begin again as soon as possible. brevity.

Having worked at a gas station that was also a service station, I had learned how to wash and detail cars, so I focused on looking for a car wash where I could practice my knowledge that I had not practiced in a long time. I didn't have to look much because a few blocks away I found one and I rushed to talk to the person in charge, who asked me to show him what I knew how to do and how quickly, my youth and energy, apart from the fact that what is learned well is not It is forgotten, but my desire to win the job made me complete the entire detail in record time and with a professional appearance, so I continued working throughout the day and would continue like this for many more weeks.

But back to that day; After having returned from work I met the young women who were already eager to start my educational advice and while I ate a delicious plate of birria I dedicated myself to explaining each of the questions they asked me, showing that I was a good advisor, so we continued until the day of the exams when I gave them my last instructions hoping that they would follow them in order. Continuing on the same day, after Anna and Dalila arrived, a conversation began and I told them about my new job and Dalila's experiences in her new job as well, although very tired we had time to pray at the request of our hosts for the way that things were happening to us and that it was surely due to divine help.

About two weeks after Dalila started working at the little restaurant, one afternoon she arrived all upset and with teary eyes, and upon seeing her that way I asked her what was the reason for her crying, so she told me that the The boss had not been satisfied with seeing her and had made indecent propositions to her, claiming that she deserved more than what she was getting from her husband. The next day I asked her not to show up for work, that I would be in charge of maintaining our expenses and that I would accompany her to receive her last salary when I left work. Just as planned at the end of my shift, I passed by her and we headed to the restaurant and without mentioning anything so as not to harm Anna, she collected what they owed her and said thank you (for whatever it was).

My efficiency at work, in addition to speaking English, had earned me that many who crossed the border to get a cheaper job and who did not speak Spanish, preferred me and left me good tips when they saw their cars in excellent shape, so we were saving more quickly what we needed. The girls had passed their exams in a very satisfactory manner, so their parents were very happy with us, but that didn't mean we stopped paying for our accommodation and the food we consumed. We had gotten names of very trustworthy people for the pass and who would charge us a reasonable price since they were acquaintances of Anna's family, so we were raising additional money to get started in Los Angeles.

After preparing the trip and saying goodbye to such a beautiful family, a new surprise awaited us; It turns out that Don Juan José had a brother who lived in Compton California and now that he had met us and how correct we were even at our young age, he decided to recommend us so that he (his brother) could help us begin our dream realization. American.

The crusade was not an easy task, because it was raining and bone-chillingly cold, and the path the guide chose was the most difficult so that the Border Patrol would be less likely to intercept us, so we suffered unspeakably. since the muddy ground made our shoes weigh a ton each and we felt that our hearts were stopping due to the emotion and the exhausting effort to which we were subjected. We had completed the first stage of the crossing by arriving at a junk car yard in Chula Vista, where a minivan would pick us up and transport us to San Diego where another person would take us to Los Angeles. They took us to a safe house (as they said) where we were picked up by a man of pleasant and distinguished appearance and with a luxurious car who would go more easily unnoticed, but not before having witnessed the most unpleasant spectacles from women who in their eagerness to crossing and not having the resources to pay, they prostituted themselves with the famous people (polleros) in front of all of us who were held there without caring who was looking at them.

The gentleman who picked us up took us directly to the house of Don Juan José's brother where he was supposed to be paid, but his surprise was enormous when, taking out the special pocket in my pants, I gave him the amount of the payment. Don Hilario came out to welcome us accompanied by his wife. They were alone because his wife Guadalupe could not have a family, but they had a very nice and spacious house to which they invited us to visit. They were not Christians, but they were very compassionate as well as very frank, so after the greetings and some questions about their nieces and their brother and sister-in-law they moved on to another topic saying: look boy, we don't bring just any people into our company. house, but in the case of my brother who called me expressly to recommend them to me, I am going to make an exception, therefore and having the room that they come to give when they visit us, I am going to give it to them free of charge for a month, after that time I will charge them An income that I will think about and if it suits us, then they will look for another place to go. Is it a deal? Of course it was a more than fair deal and we accepted it very gratefully. Then he said: well, get settled in and if you want, take a bath while Lupe prepares dinner and we eat together.

# **CHAPTER THREE**

It was her birthday and I didn't know it or I had forgotten, but it coincided with her arrival in Los Angeles, it was her eighteenth birthday and when she was alone in the bedroom she hugged me very excited and said: thank you for the gift you gave me. Given, it was my dream to be here in this country and thanks to you we have achieved it, but my happiness is double because I have at the same time the opportunity to share it with you, you are the love of my life and I promise that I will fight by your side to achieve all the purposes that come to the Land of the American Dream implies.

We were interrupted in our dialogue when we were called by our new hosts to accompany them to the dinner that smelled wonderful, that looked very good, but tasted better and the very kind gentlemen began a pleasant conversation after the appetizing dinner. And the talk was very productive because I was able to find out where I could get a fictitious Identity Card (Green Card) that they requested in most jobs. I knew that I was qualified to perform any qualified job but given the impossibility of proving my legal status, I knew that I would have to start with any opportunity that would help me fulfill the most basic commitments, so the next day after getting up very early I decided to find a source of income and I promised Delilah that she wouldn't have to worry about anything.

Don Hilario also prepared to go to work and offered to give me a direction, I accepted and asked him to please drop me off as close to the place where I could acquire the Green Card, and so he did, so after a while About two hours I was already a Legal Resident (little lies), after that I started walking in a straight line hoping to find some work on my way, I walked for about two hours and asking here, asking there and nothing. After two hours I stopped in front of a car wash that looked very busy and from what I could see they were short of employees. I approached one of the employees who answered me indirectly because I didn't want to take my eyes off the car. that he was cleaning, perhaps with the idea of not leaving a single mistake in cleaning it. I had asked him if they had any spots available so he pointed with his hand to the Manager so I could apply directly with him.

The Driver, a tall, strong and rude man, rather a dictator, addressed me in a very contemptuous manner and asked: do you know how to clean a car and drive too, to which I nodded with certainty that yes, although I did not boast of all my potential in the field so as not to be boastful, along the way I would demonstrate my abilities. After asking my name, he gave me the order to grab a basket and towels to start working immediately and I grabbed the first cart that was drying itself and the adventure began. My speed and efficiency was something that surprised the Manager, so at the end of the day he asked me where I worked before, I answered that I had just arrived and that my experience was from another place, so he challenged me by saying: see how long you can keep up that pace; to which I replied dully: we'll see, we'll see.

After trying to make friends with a couple of young Central Americans, I was heading to take a bus that I was supposed to take to get to my home, when the Manager approached me and gave me my schedule, which was going to be six days. of work for one of rest and that payday would be on Mondays, and my rest would be on Thursdays, which seemed very good to me and which I accepted. I was eager to get home to tell Dalila that I now had a job, in addition to telling her about the first tips I had received during my first hours of work.

It was quite a hard job, because what mattered was how many cars one could clean to have a better chance of adjusting one's salary with the tip. Fortunately, my youth and physical strength allowed me to do a little more than any of the workers, but nevertheless it came very tired to my home, but I did not make any comments to give confidence to Dalila who had become very sensitive and worried about everything.

It coincided that on pay day I started a conversation with the owner of the business, he of Israeli descent and with a very observant look told me: I have seen you work and I know that you have the potential for success, I would like to see how good you are at selling services because you English is very good, so we will test you tomorrow.

I arrived earlier than usual and putting my best attitude, in addition to accentuating my voice well, I dedicated myself to promoting one of the services that gave volume to the average daily sales. After finishing the day, the owner of the business dedicated himself to studying the differences in my performance and when he arrived the next day, before starting the routine, he called me to his office and made me the offer of staying permanently in the new position and He offered a tentative salary that met my expectations. This time I would have something fixed, a salary that would guarantee the payment of the commitments I made and the stability of Dalila, which was my number one priority. Although our love had become more of a Platonic love, because out of respect for the places where they had helped us we could not give free rein to our instincts, we could not express with all the strength of our bodies the explosive relationships that made us vibrate in countless orgasms, in panting dalliances that made us delirious to the maximum, expressing our names with passion, with anger and with sublimity, which led us to the doors of heaven itself.

After a month of constant work, we had to say goodbye to our hosts and friends who had already grown fond of us and asked us to stay, but our individuality was necessary to be and do what we wanted, however we promised them We visited them when we had the opportunity and we also offered our support in whatever way we could.

 We had rented a simple apartment and bought a few kitchen utensils, a bed and its accessories, it was my day of rest and I decided that everything would be properly organized, after finishing my purpose I dedicated myself to taking a long bath and then waiting for Let Dalila also do the same, while she finished cooking the dinner that she had left on the stove. She came out only wrapped in the bath towel, so my curiosity was stronger than the hunger I may have felt and taking advantage of the fact that I was also half naked I attracted her towards me, I fixed my gaze on her beautiful green eyes that seemed to me like large emeralds that They shined with the reflection of the light from our tiny lamp that decorated the headboard of the bed, I couldn't wait and without stopping to look at their eyes, as if they were an enchanted cobra, I looked for their tender and fleshy lips and began to suck the nectar from their kisses, just as if it were a hummingbird in love, like a bee that wanted to obtain honey from a delicious flower, we had lost control, we both trembled as if we were being trapped by an immense cold, but it was the desire to possess ourselves that It made our nerves and muscles tremble with the anxiety of giving ourselves to each other.

I anxiously removed from her body the towel that served as a hindrance to the purpose of possessing her and, placing her on the bed, I dedicated myself to observing her naked body, that body that would be a worthy candidate to be painted by Michelangelo's brush, that beautiful face that would be the envy of Da Vinci's Mona Lisa, and being there observing her further ignited my crazy desire to possess her, to take what for many weeks I had not been able to take in the form I wanted, to make her mine with contained passion, to feel her vibrate. her body under mine, to say her name softly and passionately, to make her vibrate in constant agonizing rattles in each of her delirious orgasms, to feel her delicate and solid breasts oppressed by my chest, until they were exhausted by so much waste of passion and fire.

Instinctively he remembered the food that was on the stove, and almost begging me he asked me to turn off the flame. I wanted to run but my strength failed me and I almost fell in the attempt, so with a good effort I accomplished my task, alone. I was able to reach a bottle of water to refresh our throats that were dry from deep breathing. And I lay down next to her to continue enjoying her perfect naked forms that made us fall again into another passionate, but this time rhythmic and sublime orgasmic event that ended when we no longer had the breath to even stay awake.

Dawn broke and we had to get up, she to prepare food for me and I to go to work after taking a bath and eating something. I promised him that I would buy him a book so he could learn English and in the meantime organize the few things we had; He hadn't finished school so I would worry about him learning the language and then finishing his studies. I was barely leaving and I already wanted to return, because just thinking about the delights of her body unnerved my mind and provoked my desire to possess her. That morning when I got to work, the owner of the business was already waiting for me, and he called me to his office again. I was worried that I wasn't doing things right, but it was the opposite, because after asking me to sit down, he started saying: you know? , I have many businesses and since my two children are studying they cannot help me at the moment, so having observed you I have convinced myself that you are a trustworthy person, I am sure that you do not have papers and I am willing to help you, so I will put you Contact my Lawyer and I will bear the expenses, the only condition I give you is that: first, that you increase my sales more and second, that you sign a three-year employment contract with some clauses that especially include your exclusivity to my business and compensation for the expenses I am incurring in case you want to undo the deal. As your responsibilities will be greater, I have thought that I will also increase your salary by an equitable and semiannual percentage. It seemed like winning the lottery, so I agreed and began to pay much more attention and enthusiasm to my work because I wanted to show my gratitude with it.

That night I arrived more excited than usual and eager to tell the new news to Dalila, who I hoped would be excited just as I was, of course she was excited and very excited she served me dinner and we ate while we made plans. Suddenly he asked me a question that made me uncomfortable, he told me: since we are not married for me it will be the same but good for you. Well I answered if you are with me anything that benefits me also benefits you, so write home and tell them that everything is going well and ask them to send you a birth certificate so you can get married and apply for your papers too and also Send them this hundred dollars, write the letter that I will spend tomorrow morning early in my lunch break.

And each one of us dedicated ourselves to writing letters, she to her family and I to Rosaura who deep down, although I didn't feel love for her, at least I was grateful for her help which was bearing fruit at this moment, Since I promised to bring her and now I knew that it would not be possible due to the care of her children, I sent her an amount of money with the promise of sending her the same amount each month so that her children could attend high school without worrying about anything. more than studying and becoming professionals.

The next day at lunchtime I went to the post office and buying the Money Orders (certified for money) I certified them so that they would arrive safely, at the same time I felt that I had done something called

Karma, which lightened my burden. soul. An overwhelming routine began, work, home and sex, it was becoming something unhealthy, something that was overwhelming Delilah, because she felt that having her once a day was not enough, plus I was turning into an Othello since I didn't want her to go out. not even to the door, because it occurred to me that in my absence he might laugh or laugh at someone else, so I started to leave the door locked.

A few weeks passed in the same situation, but now it had occurred to me that when we were making love and she was moaning with satisfaction, she probably remembered the rape and that perhaps she had enjoyed it, so one of those nights when we were in an intense and lustful sex session, it occurred to me to ask her when she was excitedly moaning with pleasure, if her moans reminded her of that experience. She immediately stopped any reciprocity in the action and told me very angrily: I never thought you would be capable of asking me something like that, but I am going to answer you and it will surely be the last time I answer such a hurtful question; Of course I did not enjoy rape in any way, although some had the matter small, there were two who had it exaggeratedly large so it was logical that when they penetrated me suddenly I would make some sound, a reflection of the impulses they made to penetrate me with violence. …and now please stay away from me because there would be no point in us making love anymore.

I felt frustrated for having caused Dalila to reject me, it was the first time someone had rejected me, but it hurt me more that she was the reason for my life, the only one who had made me feel what I believed was true love, so I begged her to forgive me and I promised her that I wouldn't do it again and I tried by all means to keep us going but it was useless, she got up and went into the bathroom and cried for about thirty minutes after which she came out. and he went to bed falling asleep, or pretending to sleep, and that's how the night passed, during which I almost couldn't sleep because of my guilt complex.

We got up as usual, he made me eat and before I left he asked me to leave him the key because he had to wash clothes, so I couldn't refuse and I left it for him asking him to be content and that we would go at night to go around to some nice place. I left saddened as well as sleepless, so I had a day of few friends, although putting on my best smile I tried to achieve a good sales average, which was my commitment.

When I left work, I went very excited to a flower shop to buy her a bouquet of Red Roses with the hope that this would make her realize how much I loved her and thus get her to forgive me. I was so excited that I didn't realize. that I had entered the apartment whistling with joy and when I stood at the door I remembered that I had left the key, when I was preparing to knock on the door I heard the voice of the building administrator who said to me: André very happy? What beautiful flowers, I didn't like the tone of his voice because I sensed that there was some sarcasm in it, so I automatically responded: yes, they are for my wife. She smiled ironically and said: well, his wife left the key here and told me to read the paper he left on the dining room table. I felt that the floor was sinking at my feet, I felt a great emptiness in my stomach, I wanted to vomit, to scream, to say something, but I didn't know what to say... I only managed to say thank you and, taking the key, I went into the apartment. and it seems that I ran towards the small dining room, in which we had eaten our meals and smiled so many times, where we made plans for everything that two young lovers used to dream of, but which was now going to be the place where I read something that perhaps It would break my life into a thousand, or perhaps millions of pieces.

The letter said: Beloved André; I know that perhaps my decision will take you by surprise, but it is because you have not realized the change that you have been having for some time, that change that you have not noticed because it has been gradual, I always tried to help you change giving you love in exchange for everything, but that made you feel arrogant and everything has a limit, there is always the straw that breaks the camel's back and you added that straw by making me feel guilty for something that was ruthless destiny that made sure that If it happens, the one who arranged for there to be a stain on my excellent reputation, but it is unnecessary to insist on trying to find culprits, I have made the decision to leave, not because I do not love you but because if we continue like this we would probably have a truly dramatic end, So I wish you the best in the world and if you find another woman, I hope she knows how to love and adore you like I did, just try not to break her heart like you did with me. Yours... in body and soul even though I am no longer with you, because I assure you I will never belong to anyone else. Delilah. PS thanks for everything.

I don't remember having cried as much as I did that night, it was a set of feelings that came from the depths of my being, it was a mixture of love, sadness, regret, guilt and many others that tormented my mind and made me They made me feel the smallest being in this world, the unhappiest I had ever imagined could exist. It occurred to me that maybe she was with a neighbor and I went out to try to hear her voice or maybe someone told me that I was alone, giving me a lesson but it wasn't like that, I went out into the street like crazy to walk around many blocks hoping to find her and I begged her to return but it was not like that, it was then that I was afraid of the pain that she could suffer and the dangers to which she would be exposed, since I did not know anyone in addition to not speaking the language, so I felt sorry for her and asked the Higher Being to He would set off on his odyssey and that one day he would be able to find her and if soon better. And I returned to the apartment, crestfallen, tearful and meditative, repentant for my cruel behavior which was the cause of my misfortune and the future of my beloved Delilah.

# CHAPTER FOUR

Dawn broke and I had to get ready to go to work, the beautiful figure of Delilah was no longer there, she was the light that illuminated my days, the one that injected me with that well-being that made me smile even on the most difficult days, the one that sweetened my coffee with her smiles and gave me encouragement to return full of energy to her side, to love her, to daydream before the spell of her gaze, to enjoy the sweet nectar of her kisses, to fall exhausted by fatigue before the passion of her sex and the delicateness of his caresses, those and other attributes were only a thing of the past.

I didn't know how to smoke or drink alcohol, otherwise I would have made a bonfire with all the cigarettes I wanted to smoke and I would have made a stream with the barrels of liquor I wanted to consume, but the misfortune I had was enough to make me want to add another to my suffering that was more than enough. And my life began to take a different direction, something that would give me many headaches as well as many satisfactions, achievements and experiences that would make me mature over the years.

Six long months had passed without me hearing from Delilah, for logical reasons my body began to demand the presence of a person of the opposite sex and it was then that I noticed so many beautiful women who came to the business and whom I attended without any interest. personal, so I decided to find someone with whom I could at least vent my animal instincts, because I was sure that I would never again be able to love someone the way I loved my beloved Delilah. It happened that it was Friday and a couple of beautiful young women arrived, who, smiling suggestively, asked me if I didn't like to go dancing, and they also boldly asked if I was married, to which I answered: the truth is, I'm not married and I've never been. to dance so I wouldn't like to make a fool of myself. They answered: we will teach you and take you to a good place, just tell us where we will pick you up and then we will return you to your house. I didn't think it was a bad idea, so I agreed and gave them my address, promising that I would wait for them at the entrance to my apartment building. It would be good to experience something new, I thought.

The day of work was over and I went to my apartment with the idea of taking a good bath and putting on one of my best clothes, so after getting ready and arriving at the established time I went out to the street to wait for the beautiful women. The taller one named Sandra was the one driving and the other, slightly shorter one named Doris was the passenger, they stopped the vehicle and after a hello, they ordered me to get in to leave immediately for the Dancing Club, I only paid my admission since the ladies did not do it, after finding a little table on the second floor of the crowded place and in which everyone was talking, shouting, getting drunk and smoking, in addition to maintaining the attitude of moving slowly throughout the entire time, as in the constant mimicry of the dance, the one who took the initiative was Sandra, who after ordering two beers and a coke for me, almost dragged me to take me to the dance floor where she began to move around as if she were stung by an anthill, it was something funny for my taste although I would have liked to be with Dalila to laugh at the event.

After doing jumps, contortions and gestures, which was what they called dancing and I had had about six cokes and they had almost the same amount of beers, it occurred to them that we had to do something extravagant and that the best thing would be for us to go to a motel, but first we went to a store to buy a bottle of something strong, as they said. After renting a room we went into it and after closing the door they pounced on me like two hungry hyenas, each one in turn began to undress me at the same time they gave me all kinds of caresses, the tallest one latched onto my the mouth with a kiss, which looked more like a suction cup that turns on and only comes off after tremendous effort, while the other one was dedicated to caressing me all over. It was something new for me, but I had no one to give accounts to so I played along and after the three of us were naked we started what seemed like a pitched battle, I was young and strong as well as a good lover so I satisfied them to the end. tired and after leaving them as if knocked out I left the place to go to my apartment in a taxi, because with two hours of sleep I would be ready for my work.

I managed to get some sleep and got up at the same time, after taking a refreshing bath I headed to work, I was tired from being sleepless but I still finished the day and thought about resting from the moment I arrived at my apartment. It was a very lonely place without the company of my beloved Delilah, I was getting emotionally ill, because not even the food had any flavor for me, I ate to eat, slept to sleep and I bathed and changed only because I had to be presentable at work. , but in reality I had lost interest in life, so much so that on my rest day I spent lying in bed listening to music from a small radio that I had bought from a co-worker who was returning to his homeland. The experience with the girls the other day had not transcended because it was something trivial, so it barely left a mark and he was sure it would not be repeated.

I wanted to find a way for Delilah to hear my thoughts, I wanted to find a way for her to know about my misunderstood love, because I loved her so much that I ended up distorting the way to make myself heard, I succumbed to the instability of my youth, I fell before the complexes of my inexperience and I was overcome by the agony of losing her since deep down I thought that I was not worthy of so much happiness.

One of those nights when I arrived all discouraged, with the vague hope of finding myself surprised to see my love sitting on the edge of the bed, reading her English book or drawing drawings in her unlined notebook, I thought I was hallucinating. Well, it seemed to me that she was really sitting there and she extended her arms to me as if offering me to hold her in mine, but closing my eyes tightly and shaking my head I came out of my hallucination to wake up to the harsh reality.

It was then that I took paper and pen and decided to write a few letters to her each day, to give myself the illusion that she was in front of me and to read them to her so that she would know how much I loved her.

## My Plea

Today that you are gone, I understand how much I love you. Now is when I want to give you my whole heart. Now that you are so far away and I haven't been able to find you. I would like to go back in time and find you at my request. Please come back, you are taking my life. Don't be mean and come back, because with your indifference you take my life.

I was not a poet but I wanted to write to him because of the impossibility of telling him face to face, I wanted to find a way to unburden my mind and live even if it were illusions. Time passed and her birthday arrived again, I remembered every detail of her, she was so sweet, loving and understanding, she was so beautiful and so beautiful, I remembered those beautiful green eyes that always looked at me with that spark of love, those lips red and fleshy that never said no to a tender or passionate kiss, the large and solid breasts that were always ready for my caresses and the hotness of her delicious sex, something that no woman had been able to match. And now my question was: Who will be delighting with such an exquisite woman? Who will be able to take care of his love and grow old by his side? Who will be able to express their love in the right way? Since I was not able to do anything to make her understand that I was wrong to express my love to her, to realize in time that I was losing her for being a fool, for not giving her the respect she deserved and for thinking that she had the obligation to accept me as I was, without understanding that she also had her ego, her ability to reason and her free will.

I kept her photograph to which I had made a shrine and that day I went to a store to buy a white candle and I lit it for her during the afternoon and prayed to the Higher Being to illuminate her path and that there would be nothing that would make her suffer because he had already suffered enough. I already had a temporary residence card and soon I would have a permanent residence card, I was achieving many things but I didn't have her to share and I think I was already losing hope of finding her even by chance, so overwhelmed by loneliness I started dating a young woman who came to wash her car accompanied by her parents, so I thought she would be a person with more emotional stability, since the previous time I had ended up disappointed by the behavior of Sandra and Doris.

Jazmín was her name, she was about five ten tall, white and brown hair, with long legs and a thin waist, large buttocks and moderate breasts, maybe thirty-eight, her face was a perfect oval decorated with large almond-colored eyes. , with long and curved eyelashes, her nose was straight in the European style and her mouth had not very thick lips with a rictus that denoted being very energetic and decorated her mouth with perfect teeth. She also dressed very discreet and elegant, so she seemed like a good candidate for something serious and that's how we started dating, although she seemed too formal for her age, since she was barely twenty-one years old.

Three months of courtship passed, although very insipid they bordered on normal, the following week after the three months had passed it occurred to me that it was time for something to happen that would be normal in our relationship, so daringly I invited her to my apartment , which although it was a simple one, it was very clean and decorated in a very modern way, by then it already had a telephone, television and some furniture that complemented the little apartment. Although there were endless excuses he ended up accepting and we went to my apartment, after offering him something to drink we opted for a couple of sodas, after a kiss and provocative caresses he ended up getting excited and already losing a little of the shame of the first time (with me) we ended up falling into the arms of Aphrodite and then I knew that her seriousness was only a camouflage of a good girl, because when her animal instinct awakened, the fire in her body was lit and she clung to me as if I were the only one who He could put it out, but he was wrong because the fire moved to me and we began to burn like two torches, like two bonfires that there was not enough water to put out.

It was a night, like the night that Rome burned, it was fire and only fire, we burned with a sordid rage as if wanting to completely merge with each other, it was desperation in each orgasm, it was an unbridled passion that had been dormant for a long time and that he wanted to let off steam in just a few hours, probably if it had lasted for another hour, perhaps we would have ended up dry as two raisins, since we evacuated our juices in torrents that wet our entire body, giving off halos of energy that invaded the apartment.

After a few hours and after enjoying the most varied positions, we were left lying on the bed as if without a soul in our bodies, all of us faint and without the strength to even open our eyes, and we stayed like that for a few minutes until gathering strength. With the reserve of energy we were finally able to sit up and speak again. Wow! He said, you are a whirlpool, you completely annihilated me, you gave me more orgasms than I could have counted, you are the best, I think that if we get married you are going to kill me in a couple of months, poor me, but I have to go then I don't want my parents to get angry, for them I am a different person and I don't want to disappoint them. So after getting ready a little in the bathroom, he left with the promise of seeing us as soon as possible, but not before he had recovered all the liquids he had lost in such a bloody but delicious battle.

What a feeling of ecstasy the meeting with Jazmín had left in me, but what a guilt complex that awoke when I realized that I had tainted the memory of Delilah, that she had been capable of committing adultery in the same bed that had been the nest. of love and the altar of sacrifices, where almost every night we worshiped Aphrodite, who accepted the rite because she knew that it was all for the sake of our immense love. Well done, but I couldn't stop feeling guilty, although that sexual encounter had been different from the one I had had before, in any case I wanted to give myself courage by saying to myself, as if justifying... I wasn't to blame, she (Delilah) he went away.

And my routine continued, only this time I had begun to think that I had to improve myself, since Jazmín was from a family of a different level than mine, although I did not feel inferior individually, I did understand that I had to improve my cultural level. and economic, to aspire to give her the standard of living to which she was accustomed. So I started to think about what career would be to my liking, quick to finish, and most productive in the short term.

I heard that the real estate market was a constant source of business and therefore a good income of dividends, since in each business one could get a good amount of dollars, at the same time I was interested in investing small capital in Mutual Funds, So on my free day I dedicated myself to studying what related to such a good and productive career and at night I talked on the phone with Jazmín and when we felt the need for the complement, she came to my apartment and we satisfied our instincts. I had begun to think with the reasoning that in reality what I felt for Jazmín was nothing like love, what I felt was the need for company and someone to mitigate my sexual desires that were constant given my youth and the abandonment of Dalila, So I began to feel a certain kind of revenge against the poor woman, who perhaps was truly feeling love.

It had all started with Delilah, because burned by the insecurity complexes that for some reason I kept in my subconscious, I had awakened in my mind the idea that she was too pretty for me, therefore I began to try to prevent any man from putting his eyes on her and made her forget that she loved me and now that she was gone because of my unhealthy jealousy I believed that my suspicions were justified, innocent poor friend I did not realize that I had been the architect of my own misfortune, but in my sick mind I reasoned that she had left me because she didn't love me anymore. And I suffered in silence trying to prove the opposite and finding a scapegoat in my new relationship and in which I had begun to avenge my frustration.

Another one of those nights, taking up paper and pen again, I tried to write to him my feelings that managed to escape from my tormentor, jealousy and my complexes and I wrote to him what my tormented soul was feeling at that moment and I said: I want you to know, my love, that now that you are gone I am like the clown who puts on his best mask to show his false appearance, but beneath it cries a wounded soul, which silently cries its tears of blood, I love you and always I will be yours...always. The crying didn't let me continue writing and I wasn't ashamed because they were true tears of love. Lost love, if as they say you live happily without me, then enjoy that happiness for both of us because I only know what sadness is and I ask heaven as my only wish not to die without first seeing your face for the last time, and I went to sleep to not continue experiencing so much sadness or perhaps to try to be happy by his side even if it were in dreams.

I really looked like the clown, because during my work hours I laughed but not to cry, because sadness overwhelmed my soul but I remained firm in my goal of self-improvement and perhaps one day I would have the joy of finding her and being able to offer her a better future. . Dreams, just that but he was sure that many dreams have come true so he would continue dreaming as long as there was hope, because hope dies last.

Two years went by without seeing her, one hundred and four weeks of missing the warmth of her body, the beauty of her person, of not looking at those big green eyes, of missing her caresses and remembering each of her details, of remembering those nights when she made me little louse so that I could fall asleep gently, little by little, and watch over my sleep until fatigue made her fall prey to it as well. The contract I had signed was about to end and I also already had my Green Card. I thought that since I had more time available, when I finished my contract and started my new profession, I would dedicate my best effort to looking for it and I hoped that everything would turn out for the best. way, although deep down I wanted it to remain just for me.

Although I continued with my promise to send money to Rosaura and through her also help my Mother, after my expenses I always had some money left that I was worried about investing in any way, the only thing that worried me was the relationship with Jazmin that it was already colder than an ice cube and every time we had an intimate relationship we always came out fighting, because everything romantic that I had been began to turn into abruptness and contempt, so one of those nights I couldn't resist anymore. and in the same way that it began, it came to an end. What difference does it make if what you never had is never missed?

I thought I needed a break, to locate myself inside to analyze what I wanted, to no longer make anyone else suffer because of my internal problems, to be happy and try to make happy whoever was next to me, even if preference wanted it to be Delilah. And I wrote a few other words to her, because I had her stuck like a thorn in my heart. I would like to have the grace to tell you beautiful things, to be able to fill with sweetness the verses that will syrup your soul, to attract the muses to ignite my imagination and to be able to tell you... I love you, in the sublime language that will subjugate your heart and make with those verses the carriage that would bring you back to me. Of course I was not a poet, but I did my best.

And he continued the routine but this time he had added something to it, he had started a bodybuilding course, because I remembered that phrase: "a healthy body, a healthy mind", also in this way I would burn excess energy, avoiding temptations at the same time. which strengthens my body and gives it a better appearance. I never imagined what could be achieved in just six months, I had burned the little fat I may have had and had gained biceps, triceps, pectorals and etc. of an enviable volume and a symmetry that had to be seen to be believed, which is why it was more sought after by the opposite sex.

I was well focused on my purposes, but who who is given bread does not eat? Well, it happened that a beautiful redhead named Nicole appeared on the scene, who I found interesting because in addition to being beautiful, she was very cultured in her communication and she also told me about her progress at the University, so it didn't seem like a bad idea to see her once. of those nights. By then I already had a stroller that my boss sold me, so I asked Nicole for an appointment and after she accepted, I went to bring her that night. We went to dinner at a nice little restaurant in the bay area, where we dined caressed by the sound emitted by the waves of the sea and a soft melody that came from a solo violin, which delighted the diners.

And so a new illusion was born in my life, she was a very pretty woman with deep feelings, her perfect oval face was adorned by her beautiful deep blue eyes, with long, curved eyelashes, her straight nose and thick, well-drawn lips. , her body was something that did not go unnoticed because her five-eleven height gave her a distinguished bearing given the elegant way she walked, and in addition her narrow waist highlighted her raised breasts and her buttocks harmonized with her long and shapely legs.

We were seeing each other for a few weeks and it seemed that we were born for each other, and so it was that one night when she felt that our relationship was on the right track, she arranged a visit to my little apartment and after some sweet and tender moments, in those of us who held hands and kissed tenderly, suddenly and as if a double personality had taken over, she began to kiss me in a compulsive and provocative way while caressing me in an erotic way, causing my reciprocity and losing respect for her. that I had kept for her until that moment, and the fire of my instinct was lit... and I began to kiss her with lust, with morbidity and I made her mine, I felt how her body merged with mine, how the heat of her belly merged. with mine and we were possessed like two madmen who could not find relief for their desires, and only the panting of two roaring beasts could be heard wanting to devour each other in a fierce battle.

We lost track of time, we forgot that there was someone other than us, we felt at times that we were levitating away from all contact with humanity and we enjoyed each orgasmic thrill that ended up relaxing our bodies and forcing us to momentary rest. She was tireless and I played along, and we continued in the bloody battle until dawn came and we were forced into a truce, which would perhaps be broken the following night, although we had both won the battle, but not the war. He had his plan prepared, because after sleeping for a couple of hours he got up and took a bath, dressed in the clothes he had brought in his handbag and went to work, but not before offering me the spectacle of seeing his freshly bathed body and admire her beauty, at the same time verify that she was a natural redhead.

When I got to work, my boss called me into the office and suggested that I continue working with him, since the contract I had signed expired the following week. I answered that I had other plans in mind and thanked him for what he had done. done for me, and in gratitude I promised to train someone to stay instead of me, although a little disappointed because he had taken a liking to me, he accepted my offer but not before assuring me that if for some reason things did not turn out as I had, I planned, the doors of his business would be open.

Luckily, a young promise had arrived, someone with the desire to do things well and with the skills to achieve it, so after two weeks of training we said goodbye. But before I got into my cart, he called me and made me come into his office and told me: André, I am very little expressive about my feelings, but for me it has been a good experience to meet a good worker like you, therefore I have decided to give you a bonus in recognition of your dedication to my company, and I think you deserve a vacation before dedicating yourself to another occupation, so here is this check and good luck to you. He shook my hand tightly and we said goodbye again.

# CHAPTER FIVE

He had given me a bonus of five thousand dollars, it was a considerable amount so I thought I would take about two days off before starting my new job, since it was Thursday I called Nicole and asked her if she would like us to spend a weekend somewhere that was to her liking, and she very excitedly asked me to go to Mammoth Lake, assuring me that I was going to love the place, a family friend of her father had a cabin in the place and at Nicole's request they ended up lending us the keys for the weekend. We left on Friday around ten in the morning, we bought some groceries and prepared to enjoy the stay. I never imagined there was such a beautiful place in the world, I remember that my homeland is very special but this landscape surpasses the imagination of any poet or painter.

We stopped at a small viewpoint, we got out of the car and sat on a mound of stones and holding hands we dedicated ourselves to observing so much beauty, the mountains with their semi-snowy peaks served as a background for the landscape, and then as the As he looked down, he came across tall, strong green and healthy pine trees, which gave way to a huge lake of blue waters that rested on a rocky bed that protruded all around in whimsical shapes of protruding rocks.

Thus we were engrossed for a long time, it was a scene that caused us to remain in memory forever, it was something that made one think of the magnanimity of the Higher Being for having built such a beautiful place for the recreation of the soul and spirit, and we were enthralled for a while longer until hunger reminded us that we had unfinished business with our stomach, and after getting back into the car we headed towards the cabin where we arrived a few minutes later.

It was a very cozy place, although everything was rudimentary, made of unpolished wood, everything still had its comfort, the only thing that was modern was the kitchen, because it had a gas stove and a refrigerator, where Nicole placed the things we had bought and began to prepare some sandwiches for a snack. The bed was made of wood but the mattress was made of springs, there was also a medium-sized television and we sat down to eat while watching the news. It was already late, so we dedicated ourselves to watching television and talking, trying to make plans for the next day, since there were many activities that could be practiced.

Everything had been going very well, until it occurred to him to start kissing me passionately and giving me suggestive caresses, which caused my excitement and the holocaust began, it was a battle in which it seemed that we wanted to exterminate each other and we enjoyed the most beautiful moments, in which that we had the wildest of sexual encounters, where we felt all kinds of sensations, from the most delicious to the most exhausting. And dawn came and we were exhausted without even wanting to open our eyes so as not to have to get up, but we gathered our will and after taking a refreshing bath and a small breakfast we were ready to go for a walk in the forest.

The curious thing was; that when we were in a sexual relationship we were very compatible, but I had begun to see things that made me think that: I wouldn't like to live with her as husband and wife because we needed that special spark of I don't know what, so when I started talking about our marriage, I changed the conversation immediately. And it had occurred to me that we would need to take some time to sort out our feelings, and I thought I would bring it up to him when we returned from the trip. We finished our excursion to such an unforgettable place and returned on Sunday afternoon, knowing that the next day my new work challenge would begin, but I was confident that I would succeed.

I had tried not to think about Delilah, but it was only when I had my mind occupied that I managed to do it, but as soon as I was alone it was the first thing that came to my mind, and the worst thing was that at times feeling that morbid jealousy, I thought that who knows? with whom I would be enjoying life while I, like a fool, suffer for it. Well, knowing that I had to show up for my new job, I opted for the healthiest option and went to sleep, but not before thinking about her for long minutes. It was dawn and after showering and eating something light, I dressed in my new clothing that included a suit and tie, so despite looking very good according to comments from the building manager who saw me when I left, I felt very uncomfortable.

It was a day of socializing, meeting other people who worked there, as well as training and studying the lists of available houses to meet the expectations of potential clients. I thought it was an interesting job and I thought I would enjoy it completely. And my first client arrived, a person who was looking for a duplex, but with my advice I sold him one with three units, so he solved his need for housing, while making a productive investment since the other unit could be rented. and thus obtain a part of the mortgage, for which he was very grateful.

It seemed to me that buying a house was not just for the sake of buying it, I was concerned about doing a small survey to determine what would best suit their needs, so I always sold them what was truly functional for them, most suitable for their budgets. and also thinking about the family future. Everything began to go smoothly, the first month I obtained the first place in sales together with another of the oldest employees of the company, which earned me congratulations from the head of the office, apart from a good check that reminded me of Delilah and begging the Higher Being that she was not suffering while I was very well.

There was no specific day off, because the more appointments I had, the more sales could be made, with the difference that I left work earlier, so I began to dedicate a couple of hours a day to visiting shopping centers and driving through the streets. aimlessly hoping to find my beloved in one of my forays. After all, I wasn't in a hurry to get to my apartment, since no one was waiting for me, because now that I had spoken with Nicole, I wasn't even waiting for her calls. And I was like that for approximately six months in which I saved a good amount of money, with which I thought about buying my house given how cheap they were, in addition to the low interest rates of the banks.

I had the opportunity to buy a small house with two bedrooms, two bathrooms and a two-car garage, the owner paid the closing costs and I had enough money left to put a little more in my mutual fund account, so I said goodbye to the house. in charge of the apartments where I lived and I begged her that if Dalila arrived she would not hesitate to give her my address and my telephone number that I wrote on a piece of paper. He was a bit of a gossip, however he was very helpful and attentive, so I thanked him with a small gift that I had bought him at a category one store.

I had not missed the opportunity to look for Dalila, because every day I went out walking the streets like crazy without a fixed direction, I stopped at each shopping center with the idea that maybe she would go out to buy something and she would cross my path, sometimes my avid The desire to see her made me mistake her for someone else, seeing her walking in front of me, and my disappointment was enormous when I saw a different face in front of me, plus the discomfort of having to apologize to the wrong woman.

One of those afternoons when I entered a supermarket, confusing her again with a beautiful woman who had all the characteristics of Delilah, I came across the almost photocopy of my beloved, they were like a copy with very few features of difference, but who woke up in I had a whole host of feelings that I thought were dormant. When I called her by the name of my beloved, she turned around and looked at me surprised, and I was even more surprised to see such a close similarity between two people, who, although they were not even relatives, had so much in mind. common, The oval of her face, the grace of her little ears, the beautiful and big eyes and the draw of her eyebrows, her hair was the same... wavy and black and her lips thick and fleshy, her body reminded me of the overflowing curves of Delilah Like the rest of his body, the only difference was the color of his eyes, which had a caramel hue.

Seeing her so close to me I hesitated, I felt very confused and I couldn't articulate a word, so she, who was obviously very outgoing, deigned to ask me to calm down and take my time, if I wanted to ask her something, I Still hesitant, I asked her to apologize and that I only intended to ask her about a mutual friend, the person I had confused her with. After the scare and as if wanting to restore my confidence in me, he decided to start a small talk that became very interesting when we realized that we had a lot in common. Her name was Leticia, secretary of a Real Estate company, which I found out after a few minutes and I therefore provided her with information about me. We talked for a few more minutes and after giving her one of my business cards I asked her to He would call me when he wanted to talk or go out for maybe an aperitif or an informal dinner.

A week passed without me hearing from her, but one of those afternoons around five o'clock, when I was about to go home after a hard day of work, I received a call from Leticia who sounded very excited and as if sobbed, now I was the one who suggested calm and asked her to meet somewhere that seemed appropriate to her, so we agreed to meet at a restaurant that she chose and that was not far from me, so in question In minutes I was at the place and where she arrived a few minutes later. She was very upset and with teary eyes, apart from her hair disheveled, so asking her to sit down and asking her what she would take, I asked her to tell me what had happened to her.

Falling back into her bitter tears, she began her story, but not before grabbing one of my hands, which she squeezed tightly and began saying: please don't make fun of me, but in reality I don't have trusted friends who can help me in this dilemma. that I have, just six months ago I met a man a little older than me who gave me very nice gifts and asked me to marry him, so believing everything he said I fell for his lies, but what would be my disappointment when by chance his wife arrived at the office where I work and when filling out some documents she put his name, and by coincidence also his cell phone number, the truth was not so much about his gifts, because the nice thing was the details What he had to give them to me or to take me a bouquet of flowers, for which I had fallen in love, and now realizing his deception...I don't know what to do.

In truth, it was a very common story, since man, in his macho instinct, takes pleasure in conquering whoever is most susceptible to conquest, but in this case in particular it affected me greatly, since Leticia saw herself as a woman with noble and noble feelings. Because of the great resemblance to my beloved, I was even more upset since I imagined that it could be Delilah who was suffering for a Don Juan. In the depths of my soul I asked the Higher Being to take care of her and protect her from pain like the one poor Leticia was suffering. So analyzing my words I tried to encourage her and urged her to try to focus her mind on something that would get her out of that rut in her path and that in time she would have the opportunity to fall in love with someone worth giving her love to. .

After talking for a long time in which I advised her in a thousand ways, she felt much better and told me: how happy your wife must be to have such an understanding man and she looked me in the eyes as if wanting me to answer her. to her doubt, but I did not intend to take advantage of the situation, on the contrary I offered to help her overcome that bad situation in which she was at the moment, and that one day I would tell her about my life, but that the most important thing was that to move away from that unhealthy relationship, and if for some reason she kept any of those gifts, she would return them so as not to feel committed in any way to the liar.

Now more serene, she said goodbye to me, and after getting into her car, she gave me one last look and these words: I knew I could count on you, my heart was not wrong... I'll call you later, and she probably went home and I I did the same because I had to deliver accounts to Morpheus. I got up early as usual, after my refreshing bath and having a light breakfast, which consisted of cereal with milk and a peanut butter sandwich, I headed to work where I had to receive some potential clients for a property. Having met Leticia had motivated me, I felt that I had recovered a good percentage of my love, so I put my best effort into presenting the property, I got the purchase request signed and I only had to wait a few days for the closing sales.

I couldn't stand it and since I already had Leticia's phone number, I called her when I thought she was no longer at work. When she answered and recognized my voice, she told me that she was already doing what I had advised her and that she felt very sorry. Better yet, I just had to face him to tell him the truth and give him back his things, but he would like us to talk one of those afternoons and maybe he would invite her to the movies to get rid of the bad taste in his mouth... that is, if my wife didn't hit me; so I had to clarify to him about my forced singleness.

The week passed without major incidents, I only received a call from her to tell me that she had already put him in his place and that she was trying to restructure her life and her feelings, because she did not want to fall into the hands of another liar again. She wanted to find a friend she could trust, without the double intention of a freeloader who could find easy prey in a woman hurt by the pain of lying. I couldn't deny that I liked her, but I also didn't like the idea of being a freeloader, so I preferred to give her time and help her get out of that bad situation.

We had been new friends for three weeks, and we talked from time to time about things related to his work or mine, but one of those afternoons when the weekend was approaching, he dared to invite me to go dancing, in In reality I was not a good dancer, I had not even liked the idea of going to a dance center, but with the exception of my poor ability to dance, I accepted the invitation, however I warned him that if for some reason I did not feel At ease in the place, we would have to leave there immediately to which she agreed.

The long-awaited weekend arrived, and she in her car and I in mine headed to the place that she had selected and where upon arriving I discovered that it was very beautiful, in addition to playing a Caribbean Orchestra that had everyone dancing to happy music. tropical. The rhythm was contagious and reminded me of my homeland, with its cheerful coastal atmosphere, where everything is joy despite the vicissitudes of so many people due to poverty. But we were there to enjoy the night, so as soon as we found a table and ordered something to drink, we started dancing, forgetting about any sorrow we might have had.

We danced until dawn, we danced until we were tired and we enjoyed the night, what I liked about her was her spontaneity, in addition to that spark of joy that she kept in her beautiful eyes in which I could read all the sublime of her soul, and in which he was telling me that he was beginning to like me and that although he was afraid to love me, he wanted to accept the challenge. My experience in love told me; that it was not yet ripe to cut that delicious apple, so making her wait a little I promised her that we would go out the following week and that we would make some changes to make it more exciting. He didn't like the idea much, and reluctantly had to accept, in addition to having no options.

The following week she had me harassed by phone in the morning and afternoon, telling me how anxious she was for the expected day to arrive, and I, very patiently, also responded the same, since she had already awakened in me the desire to love her. She was a very liberal young woman, although she had very defined self-esteem and decency, and like everyone in life sometimes makes mistakes, she had also made mistakes with that liar, but that was not important to me, because I did not know her. when that happened, so I prepared myself for a night full of joy and dancing.

It was a delight to see her move her delicious curves and her voluminous breasts to the rhythm of the lilting notes of the music, something that awakened morbidity in my lonely mind, which had already lost hope of finding my beloved Delilah. So I resigned myself to the idea of enjoying the moment with Leticia, as long as there was an opportunity to be by her side. We had arrived early to have more time to enjoy, so when midnight arrived we were already a little tired, so I suggested that we go have something to eat and maybe have a glass of good wine, which she very much accepted. pleased with the detail.

I took her to a discreet but elegant restaurant in the Long Beach area, and after waiting to be seated I ordered a delicious bottle of Chardonnay which was served at its cooling point, although I was not a big lover of alcoholic beverages I had learned to select a good wine, while also enjoying it very occasionally given the new relationships he had and with whom he spent some time on business matters. We ordered seafood, I think she had scallops with lobster cream, and I had halibut with almond cream... she kept looking at me, so much so that I thought she was eating poorly, so I invited her to eat and then we would look at each other as much as she wanted , so he laughed for a few seconds.

 We enjoyed the dinner to the fullest and we talked about many topics with the intention of getting to know each other more deeply, or with the intention of doing an analysis of each other's personalities, I personally liked her a lot and I wanted her in the same way that I wanted Dalila during a long time. We talked about our childhood, adolescence and our young adulthood and we agreed that we had too many things in common, therefore our planned relationship would have a high chance of lasting. Before asking her to be my girlfriend, I made it clear to her: that I didn't want us to touch on the topic of the liar for any reason, and that we were completely honest with each other and vice versa.

When we left the restaurant we walked under some trees that were in the parking lot, it was a moonlit night and we dedicated ourselves to observing her under the shadow of the largest tree and there with all the romanticism as a framework I asked her to be my girlfriend, she was She smiled very excitedly because she didn't think I was so serious and at the same time so romantic, so she somewhat excitedly told me yes, that she would love me with all the strength of her heart, as she had already begun to do.

I promised her that it would be just for her, and that my love had all the seriousness to end it at the altar, and to form a beautiful family. She offered me her lips and we fell into a passionate kiss, which took me back to one of those beautiful moments with my beloved. I immediately withdrew from her when I thought of Delilah, because I didn't want my love to be in the body of another. the illusion of my beloved. I wanted to possess her but it seemed too fast, but she was very modern and asked me to take her to my house to get to know each other better, better?  I insisted, don't you think it's very fast? To which she replied; what is going to be tomorrow, let it be today.

We arrived at my little house, and using the remote control I opened the garage, going first to show her where she could park. Then I opened the front door for her to come in, and after closing the door behind me... she was surprised to see how well-equipped the room was, in addition to the taste in decoration, then I took her to the kitchen and part of the backyard, leaving Lastly the bedroom. We passed the bedroom unnoticed, perhaps so that there would be a different feeling if we owned her, and we headed to the living room to get rid of the cold of the relationship, "make yourself comfortable," I told her and we took off our shoes, and we huddled on the sofa where We began to kiss tenderly.

We were starting to burn, so she asked me to excuse her for a few minutes, heading to the bathroom, where she came out minutes later with a fresh mouth and with the button of her blouse open, now the one who asked for time was me heading to the same place. , I came out with a clean mouth and a little perfumed and we continued what we had started, those tender kisses were the spark that would light the bonfire, because they became kisses of passion, of fury, of desire to possess us to the point of exhaustion, and My expert hands began to slide over all parts of her beautiful body, to run my manly hands all over her back until I reached her bulging buttocks, to feel like a baby sucking her tender nipples that I delicately tasted with my burning tongue, to caress her sliding movements from her heels, to the slender shape of her waist, and then lower my naughty fingers over her vulva, caressing the silky beauty of her mons, in soft and warm decoration.

We couldn't take it anymore, so lifting her up from the sofa we headed to the bedroom, after turning on a lamp that left a semi-darkness in the room, I gently laid her down to remove the last clothes that were a hindrance to achieving our desired body-to-body union. . Being with my manhood excited to the maximum, I hesitated for a moment to admire the exquisite anatomy that he had, to explore one by one all the angles of his delicious body, which I was going to possess, I felt his expressive gaze that told me; Don't be late, I'm melting with desire for you to possess me, and I didn't make her wait any longer, taking her shapely legs that I raised to the height of my shoulders and slid them to the sides, leaving her juicy, pinkish vagina exposed, which I penetrated. gently and slowly, I had all the time in the world, so why hurry! But she couldn't stand my slowness and gaining momentum with her torso she pushed herself towards me, causing complete penetration, what a delight! She had a warmth that is rare in women, it was a fire that provoked my excitement to the maximum, she kissed me deliciously, at the same time she writhed under me, causing a rare and difficult to forget joy.

It was intoxicating to hear my name, pronounced with that accent of supplication or ecstasy...André my love, oh what a delight...please move more...please, I knew you were going to make me happy...more, more, more. I had no notion of time, I only know that it was a delight to be there making love to each other, listening to her pleas and sighs every time she had an orgasm, which we repeated countless times, on behalf of both of us, because we both enjoyed the pleasures of love. It was dawn and we had to get up, she had to show up at her house and tell a white lie to her parents, so that they would at least feel "respected", so we said see you soon, but hoping it wouldn't be so soon because of the fatigue of which we were prey.

After saying goodbye to her at the door of my little house, I went to take a resuscitating bath, and I was scared when I saw my face in the mirror, I looked like a zombie activated by voodoo, because I had dark circles under my eyes that were scary, so I dedicated myself to sleeping for a few hours more, deep down in my soul I felt that I had recovered Dalila, with the difference that she was now more ardent than before, also outgoing since she let me know what she was feeling, at the same time that she was more active in the lovemaking moments. , and the most notable thing was the temperature of her vagina, which made me lose my mind and maintain a constant erection.

But there was something that I began to analyze, it was the lack of sweetness that Dalila radiated in contrast, that tenderness that was part of her idiosyncrasy, the sweetness of her voice, the melodiousness of her expressions and how attentive and helpful at all times, but I thought quickly; There are no two glories together! After having slept a little more, I dedicated myself to writing some letters to Rosaura, she had been the basis of who I was, therefore I could not forget my commitment to raise her children, so when I sent her her money I also wrote to her telling her about small events in my life and urged her to rebuild her life, because it would not be good for her to grow old without someone to share her life with her.

I received a call from Leticia, she was very excited and asked me a provocative question: do you think our love life will be the same after we get married? Well, if so, maybe it will only last a couple of years...ha, ha, ha. I replied: I'll see what I can do to make you put up with me for at least four, ha, ha, ha, and we agreed to see each other in the middle of the week, but that we would be in contact by phone, but not before making one last observation about me. skill making love and the generosity of me….

And the routine returned, although it was something very different from other jobs, because every day I met different people who made being in the office fun. They say that with the same yardstick you measure you will be measured, and it happened that in the same way that I treated Delilah during the last months and that caused her escape, in addition to my constant suffering which I was trying to mitigate with the presence of another woman . Returning to the payment of my guilt, it turns out that Leticia was beginning to collect the bill from me, because she began to become possessive, jealous and inquisitive, which was making me see how Dalila felt in her last months at my side, I felt sorry for her. her and I regretted not being able to remedy the damage that I had caused her with my wrong behavior, in addition to reawakening in me the desire to continue looking for her and I decided to start my search again, in addition to talking to Leticia regarding her behavior, which was leaving much to be desired. of an intelligent and modern woman.

That last day of her impertinent calls, which I did not answer, was the one that served to plan my strategy, so the next day and first thing in the morning when I was thinking of calling her, immediately after picking up the phone I heard her voice and the beginning of her complaints and questions. , to which I immediately stopped forcefully and told him that we had to talk and that he should not call me until we had started a conversation about older people.

We had agreed to meet at my house during the night, so after she arrived I asked her to sit in the living room and I offered her something to drink. She was very angry so I asked her to calm down because we were people with enough judgment and that we could fix any situation so as not to fall into impasses. She was red with anger and tried to start the dialogue by complaining to me about why I hadn't answered the phone all day. I wanted to reason with her by explaining that; Our young relationship was in its most difficult stage and that we had to be prudent in our expectations and our behavior, since impertinences and baseless arguments would not take us anywhere, in addition to this stage would set the pace that our relationship would have in the future. the future.

She was a person with multiple personality, because suddenly she started sobbing asking me to forgive her, because she felt very alone and wanted to feel my support even if it was over the phone. I had always believed in a second chance, so after giving him some advice on how we would best handle our relationship, we ended up reconciling on our throne of love. Despite everything, I was beginning to realize that our relationship was founded on her resemblance to my beloved Delilah, so I believed that she only served as a pretext to idealize my love for the other, the true one...the only one.

Although she filled the void in my life, at times I felt a certain aversion to her way of acting, since it was not the same as her physical resemblance to Dalila. Leticia was more materialistic and never agreed with the opinions of others, except for my comments that he accepted more out of complacency than approval. It was becoming a relationship that only fulfilled our sexual instincts, which was the only affinity that I thought we had, because apart from that sometimes the situation became unsustainable, which was leading me to a blunt decision and that perhaps was going to provoke him. more pain to her than to me.

I had made a decision and I had always been energetic about them, so I asked Leticia to meet in a small park that was near her house, so that I wouldn't have the excuse of ending up tangled in my bedroom again, since everything had gone beyond the limits. tolerable, plus I believed that a relationship should be founded and lived based on love. As night fell and very surprised that I was meeting her in a public place, she came promptly to the appointment that was anticipated to be dramatic and full of reproaches and insults, but for which I was prepared with convincing and irrefutable arguments.

After explaining to her the reason for the appointment, and that it was nothing more than to break up our relationship that had lasted barely four months, she rushed at me angrily, shouting all kinds of expletives, and grabbing me by the collar of my shirt, she pulled it, tearing off two buttons from the shirt. I immediately took her hand with one of mine, while I instinctively protected myself with the other, managing to free her from my shirt and stepping back, I left her talking and blaspheming, quickly moving away to avoid a major incident. On the way home I thought; I was right to end that unhealthy relationship in time that would not lead us to a good end.

And to continue life, to enjoy it in another way, in which there were no problems that would make it disastrous, so I focused on my favorite hobby, to strengthen my body and to search for Delilah as far as possible. I don't know why the problems insisted on following me, was it because I had the ability to solve them? Or because they took pleasure in making my life difficult? I don't know, but one of those days a family of four showed up with intentions. to buy a house from our property list, the couple in their forties and with two beautiful daughters, Elena eighteen and Jessica twenty-four, who deeply caught my attention, because when we crossed eyes we felt (or I felt) that crush of love for first sight, and when we took them to check out the property we took the opportunity to start a very short chat.

After having toured the property and agreeing with it, they asked me for a day to make a decision and in the meantime not to offer it to anyone else, I agreed and gave them my business card, but she asked me for an additional one, arguing that it could be lost. That happened in the morning and around five in the afternoon, I received a call and it was nothing more than Jessica, telling me that she liked the way I treated people and that I should clear her doubts, so I asked Which is it? She answered, are you married? I denied it and, very excited by the tone of her voice, she told me: see you tomorrow!

They arrived around ten in the morning and went straight to the point, I filled out all the papers and let's start the business, we will keep the house they said, so I started everything related to the business, but without taking my eyes off the eyes of Jessica, who had me spellbound with that analyzing and suggestive look. After finishing the business paperwork, which would take a few days to complete, they said goodbye and before leaving she approached me asking if I had plans for the weekend. I told her the truth, so she promised to call me before weekend, I agreed, but not before reasoning how liberal the girls are in this country.

It was a family with a comfortable economic situation, as well as a very good education, as I was able to analyze by the way they acted and treated people. So I was thinking about Jessica all afternoon and evening, I felt guilty for having interrupted my thoughts about Delilah, but I couldn't live on memories, but I didn't lose hope of finding her and then it would be different, or maybe by then I no longer felt what I felt at that moment... I was beginning to falter in the perseverance of my feelings, because at first I was only interested in my sexual satisfaction, but now I was beginning to feel something deeper. What was happening to me?

I felt confused, I was not able to understand what Jessica had been able to awaken in me, the image of Delilah appeared in my mind, and I remembered one by one her physical and moral details, and perhaps intellectual, but especially what pious of her soul, I remembered the time she was eating a cupcake and she began to remove pieces of it and sprinkle them around a tree in a small park in our town, I asked her why she was doing it and she answered me; The little ants are hungry too.

Suddenly, as if in competition, the image of Jessica appeared to me and I began to remember her beautiful face, the perfect oval with those pretty brown eyes, adorned by her long eyelashes and her well-plucked light brown eyebrows, her straight and small nose. , her mouth was a little wide with thick, fleshy lips and decorated with white, well-distributed teeth that gave her a perfect smile, her chin was a little prominent that gave her that dominant look, but I hoped it wasn't like that, she was tall so she stuck out. the long and well-shaped legs, with a narrow waist and wide hips and a bust of reasonable dimensions, perhaps a size 38, and in addition, lush natural brown hair that fell below her shoulders.

It was a powerful reason for me to have been captivated by such an exquisite woman, but the most important thing was; that I was not indifferent to her, so I waited to see what fate had in store for me, to whom I had asked to let luck be the one to direct my life, but who had taken it upon herself to meddle in everything, in good and bad, but in any case I had no way of keeping him away from my life and from the people who crossed my path. So I waited patiently for the weekend to arrive.

And since there is no deadline that is not met, nor day that does not arrive, on Friday around four in the afternoon I received the long-awaited call. Shall I speak to Mr. André? I immediately recognized her voice and answered: yes, Miss Jessica, it's me, how can I help you? Don't be so formal, just call me Jessica, do you have time to talk? Of course yes, I replied. Well, I have some questions to ask you regarding the house we are buying and I would like to invite you for a drink while we discuss those points. Could you come to the Mall del Amo around six? There is a cafe on the second level. I'll wait for you. ? Of course I will be there, see you soon…. and we hung up.

# CHAPTER SIX

I left at that same moment and headed home with the idea of taking a bath and changing my clothes and putting on a little perfume, I wanted to make a better impression, I didn't want to disappoint her. I arrived promptly at six, for me punctuality means; neither before nor after, but she was already sitting there waiting for me and when I commented on my punctuality, she answered me; He didn't arrive on time, because I told him around six o'clock, ha, ha, ha, and we laughed in unison. She looked so elegant dressed in that beautiful modern-cut dress in a pink tone with wide transverse gray stripes, with black shoes as well as her small patent leather party bag, her seductive lips were painted fuchsia, which They made them more seductive.

After we sat down, I asked him what he wanted to drink and after ordering the conversation began; After introducing myself correctly, I asked her for her full name and the exact reason for her invitation to said shopping center. She answered me in a very simple way, telling me her full name and the special reason for the invitation. To begin with, I do not want you to misinterpret my behavior because my invitation is because I have a doubt, it turns out that when I met you you seemed like an interesting person, because your way of speaking and the confidence with which you carry yourself is very admirable, your demeanor Your dashing appearance and your athletic body create an impression of security when dealing with you, but deep in your eyes a ray of contained sadness appears and you feel that halo of melancholy when trying to feign complete happiness. I'm about to finish my studies in Psychology and I became interested in you to try to help you in some way to get the problem you may be facing out of your mind.

At first I felt some frustration when I heard the reason for the invitation, but then I reconsidered and accepted the good intention of his purpose, but I assured him that I had no problem and that perhaps it was his imagination that made him see that. And he said, let me ask you a few questions if you don't mind, will you? To which I agreed, a little annoyed, but I tried to hide it. He began by asking questions about my childhood and if I had been happy, if I had a wife and children, and if I had no financial problems, to which I answered honestly, trying to be as concise as possible in my answers.

He had a little notebook in which he wrote every detail of our conversation, which had become very annoying, and was going off on a tangent, so I hastily suggested that we change the subject and that he tell me something about it, paying attention. Ignoring my suggestion, he continued writing for a few more minutes, until he suddenly looked at me intently and concluded; I know that your strong character prevents you from showing how noble your heart is, but deep down you suffer for not having realized any of your dreams, and that is why you can see that little drop of sadness in your eyes that tarnishes your happiness, even if you deny it. . I wanted to make fun a little to downplay the certainty of her observation, but in my mind I recognized that she was absolutely right, but I still tried to downplay the matter and invited her to taste her coffee.

After taking a few sips, she returned to the topic, and that was when she promised me that she was going to help me regain the happiness that I needed and that she would be my friend when I wanted to tell her about any of my frustrations, and give me the appropriate solution to the problem. problem. Without her wanting it, she was opening the wound that my soul carried and that did not heal even with the passing of the years. So after about an hour of an uncomfortable conversation for me, we said goodbye and she promised that we would see each other again. When I got home it occurred to me to write a few more letters to Dalila, to remind her that I still loved her as always. It is not the lack of light or shadow, it is the lack of your presence that accelerates the uncertainty of my soul, it is not the lack of bread or water, it is the lack of your presence that prevents me from mitigating my hunger for love, yours forever.

I, who had gone out with the hope of having a good time and forgetting about my loneliness, which was my worst enemy, had returned worse than how I was after my breakup with Leticia, so I went straight to bed, to at least stop thinking about what was hurting me. I could hardly sleep, I had nightmares and woke up constantly, so the dawn was a relief for me, I woke up sleepy but I motivated myself with a good coffee and some toast with jam and I got ready to watch a little television to forget about everything even if it was for a moment, fortunately I found a cowboy movie and disconnected my mind from all problems.

The beginning of the week arrived again, so I prepared my suit and everything related to start the week, I had received some calls regarding new properties and I focused on what was my main purpose, selling houses and realizing the dream of some people….the American dream. Upon arriving at my office, I found the lists and began to memorize in order to find the right property for the needs of potential clients, and compare with the requests of those who had called me in my absence.

I was very enthralled in my work when I received the call from Jessica, she wanted to apologize for the bad time she had probably given me by trying to help me with my "possible problem", and she wanted us to meet again but in another place and forget about her profession and mine, naturally it had to be like that, because otherwise and no matter how pretty and beautiful she was, she would surely not go on any dates, so I assured her that we would see each other during the week and that I would call her, she asked me a little confused, are you upset? To which I replied: of course not, but I have a lot of work accumulated and I have to finish it, so please be a little patient and I will invite you to dinner one of these nights, will you? I'm waiting for your call, take your time.

On Wednesday I called her around ten in the morning, I knew that she was studying in the afternoon and that at that time she would be home, her mother answered, to whom I greeted and assured that the bank was about to finalize the loan documents, she She thanked me and asked me if I wanted to talk to Jessica, so I thanked her for the gesture and waited for her to pick up the phone and we started the conversation. Hello Jessica, I promised I would call you and I always keep my promises. Do you want to go to dinner today? ? I know a nice place on the seashore, what do you think if I stop by for you? She replied very excited, but that she couldn't go until Saturday, since she had to attend classes in the afternoon and left after ten at night, so if I didn't mind, we would leave it for Saturday after seven, and not having a valid argument, I accepted, wishing him a good day.

I was thinking about Jessica's qualities, she was a person with refined habits, she had class, in addition to being happy and cultured, very intelligent since it was not necessary to give many explanations for her to understand the meaning of the talk or the intention of the sentences. . And my busy schedule continued, serving clients and doing my best to give my best. Until the long-awaited weekend arrived and with it the hope of taking Jessica to dinner, although I had not lowered my guard regarding the search for Delilah, although sometimes I asked myself, and for what? Well, there were several reasons, first ; to know why he had left without even saying goodbye, and second; to be able to help her if necessary and show her how much she had made me suffer.

Well, I hadn't been successful, but I had to distract my mind and therefore I went to pick Jessica up from her house, to take her to dinner at a nice place by the sea, it wasn't ostentatious but it was very romantic, well The lights were very dim and there was a piano and violin duo, which delighted the loving diners. She was very elegant, dressed in a black dress with light rhinestones on the front and with a discreet neckline in the front and back, her tiny lizard skin bag and red mid-heeled shoes, she was wearing ruby earrings, as is the heart-shaped ruby pendant on her neck. I dressed in a modern Oxford-colored suit, gray shirt and tie, and black shoes. We made a nice couple, a couple of older gentlemen who were leaving the establishment told us.

After agreeing to have meat for dinner, we ordered a bottle of a delicious Spanish red wine produced in Catalonia, (Clos Mogador) enjoying his company, the dinner and the romantic melodies that prepared us for romance. It was an unforgettable evening, and to top it all off I asked her to take a walk along the rocky view of the ocean and already very close to each other I asked her: do you have plans to fall in love? To which she replied: I didn't have them, but my thinking has changed, because a handsome and intelligent man came into my life and is keeping me up at night. I asked her: I know you don't know much about me, but would you like to be my girlfriend? and you will get to know me little by little. She answered very excited: I feel like I already know you and I do want to be your girlfriend and I want us to be immensely happy.

And we fell into a long and passionate kiss that lasted for endless minutes, but that seemed like a few seconds to me, which we interrupted when she felt like she was drowning and half suffocated and she told me: you really know how to kiss, what a delight of Kiss! And we were there for a long time, holding hands and kissing while we watched the crescent moon, which served to make our evening more romantic. We had to go back, but now there was a new hope, so after saying goodbye at the door of his house with a long and sweet kiss, we promised to contact him the next day.

It was a night of castles in the air, of illusions, of dreams that did not let me sleep, and longings that this time I could be happy for a long time, and I was like that for many hours, until finally fatigue took over me. I force myself to sleep. I woke up in an enviable mood, and after taking a good bath and putting on sports clothes, I called Jessica to see if she wanted to take a walk along the beach in Redondo Beach and maybe eat at a restaurant on the pier there, which she didn't like. It seemed like a bad idea and after picking it up we didn't go there, with the joy and enthusiasm of two newly lovers. After arriving and parking the car, we headed to the beach and taking off our shoes we began to walk along the warm sands, occasionally wetting our feet with the cool waters. It was a wonderful afternoon, which we ended with a snack at a restaurant located on the pier and which had a wonderful view of the sea.

I thought: how nice it is to be in love, especially with a young and beautiful woman, also beautiful and intelligent, I couldn't get enough of the emotion and I decided to do my best so that our relationship would last for endless years. After leaving her at the door of her house, I headed to my house to try to put everything in order to start the work week, but not before promising to communicate by phone during the week. I felt like a kid with a new toy, and I wasn't able to think about anything other than Jessica, so my motivation was at its highest, so during that week I became number one in sales, which It earned me a very significant monetary prize.

I received letters from time to time thanking me for the financial help, but almost never a loving word, neither from my family nor from Rosaura, who perhaps had already forgotten me but who in the end had gotten used to it. Anyway, I credited the prize to my bank account, hoping that it would pay dividends for our future with my new love…..Jessica.

Three wonderful months passed of a clean and pure love, of a mystical relationship in which morbidity did not exist, where the union of our souls was neat, without sin and without stain and that dignified us as exceptional beings and we felt immensely happy. . But the good lasts, until the bad appears and it happened that one of those afternoons, a Saturday when we had gone to dinner and drank a little more than normal, euphoria and irresponsibility took over us and morbidity and bad intentions entered my brain, making me act like a real animal, inducing me to provoke and demonstrate my qualities as a good lover.

Poor thing, she was not able to resist my Machiavellian kisses, the tricks of my caresses and my use of her most sensitive parts that I knew how to touch, I made her melt like butter in front of the hot knife, I had taken her to my little house with the intention of consummating my evil desires, to possess her, to feel those repressed desires on her part, to unleash the maelstrom of passion that I had had inside me for a long time, waiting for the opportunity to release her and give free rein to all her momentum, to overflow all my manhood saved for a few months, and it was time for it to overflow in a torrent of manly juice, until it achieved its objective, which was to satisfy and be satisfied.

We didn't have time to take off our clothes, it was a lightning delivery in which only the sound of our suffocated breaths was heard, the sound of our hearts beating in an extremely agitated way, of listening to the slap of our sexes when they bumped against each other. the other and we succumbed to the influence of Aphrodite or I don't know which of the Mythological Gods, and there we were left side by side, looking at each other's faces as if scared of what had happened, with this guilt complex on her part and with satisfaction to the surface on my part.

What a pity! It shouldn't have happened! She said, and covered her face with her hands, and cried for a few minutes as if she wanted to pay with her tears for the sin she had committed, but I was there to console her and tell her that it had been normal for two who love each other and who have plans. to form a family, of two young souls who had to complement their great love, and had no choice but to enter into resignation and continue the second stage of our moment of morbidity. This time, after kissing her again with the most expressive way of kissing, I began to remove the covering that prevented my curiosity from becoming more intense, which prevented me from seeing in detail the beauty of her body, the bulk of her shapes and the natural fragrance of her. a young woman, who, by emanating her natural pheromones, ignited my animal instincts which turned me into an insatiable lover who asked for more and more.

And we were there for a long time, I don't know how long... But it was enough to leave her extremely dehydrated, just like me, because when we came to our senses from our wild attitude, we realized that we needed water, a lot of water to quench our thirst. that preyed on us. It had been a hand-to-hand fight, an unbridled madness that made us prey to the most amazing orgasms, the most shocking and delirious moments, which transported us to unknown dimensions and in which we learned about the undiscovered side of love.

We were exhausted but with our senses active, admiring the physical qualities, the masculine to the feminine and vice versa, and we felt attracted again and fell into another moment of overflowing sexual activity that filled us with complete satisfaction and turned us back into normal beings, which They no longer wanted to fall into morbidity, at least not for that day, and we devoted ourselves to complimenting each other of different kinds, and which highlighted each other's attributes.

For that day it had been enough, she had a nice car, but it was a mutual agreement that I should bring her home in mine, so after getting ready a little, I took her to her house, where she was already Her mother was waiting for her at the door, since it was very late at night. I had to apologize for taking her so late, but I argued that the car had had problems, and I promised that it wouldn't happen again. I was an adult woman, but I was a little old-fashioned, so I always asked for the consent of their parents for important things.

It had been a delicious delicacy that I had devoured the night before, and I didn't want to stop thinking about it, so, taking me out of my delicious memories, my boss asked me if I was feeling well, so I answered: yes, very good boss, do you need something? I didn't just think there was something wrong with you ha ha ha. At around twelve in the morning, I received a call; She was the one who had slept late without having proposed it and she wanted to know if I also felt as tired, of course I answered but I had no choice but to come to work, do you want to meet today? I asked, to which she hurriedly replied: no, I think I won't go to class because I feel terrible, we'll talk to each other tomorrow, do you think? Which I accepted immediately, because my animal instinct had been satiated to the max and I didn't want any more of that for a few days.

I also wanted to recover the energy I had wasted to the maximum, and try to continue with my bodybuilding routine and the performance of my work at its best level, so that night I went to bed earlier than usual, to be Ready first thing the next day. My routine was an hour and a half to two hours maximum, and from six am to eight am maximum, so I had time to take a shower and enjoy a delicious fruit juice and protein before going to work.

I left work at four thirty in the afternoon, so at five I was already home, while I prepared my meals I watched television to keep up with the news, after eating I dedicated myself to reading literary works and sometimes novels of different genres, in order to maintain a good vocabulary and spend my time on healthy things. But on Tuesday afternoon when there was a knock at the door, I was surprised to see Jessica when she opened the door. It was a pleasant surprise, but not expected, so I asked her if something was wrong. She, a little angry, replied: Can't I visit her? my boyfriend? So I hurried to answer: of course yes, but you surprised me, please come in.

I invited her to sit down and asked her if she wanted to have something to drink, so she accepted a cup of coffee that I had just made and that smelled very good, but not before approaching me and giving me a long and suggestive kiss, and offering me some praise for my application in the amatory arts. We settled down in the dining room and began to talk about trivial things, without any significance, and then fell into the topic that interested us and that had something special. I want you to know: that I have always been very reserved with the opposite sex and that my intention was not to fall easily into sexual matters, first because I respect myself, and second because I wanted the day we got married to be exciting, But having gone through what happened, I'll have to be more careful when you ask me out, it's not true! I want to say that I will start a contraceptive method, to avoid a complication in our relationship, which at the moment I believe is not very stable, despite having had sex.

Know? I had always dreamed of finding a man like you, strong, intelligent, good-looking, and with noble feelings like the ones I have found in you, I want you to know that there has only been one other man in my life, we were going to get married, but by chance Bad luck, he enlisted in the Army and left without saying anything and that was three years ago, it seems that he didn't take me very seriously, because not even his family could tell me anything about him. I well believe that things happen the way they do for a reason, which neither you nor I can understand, but which has been for our benefit. Don't think that I am an easy woman because I succumbed to your charms, but the truth is that you would have to be made of wood not to reciprocate the delight of your caresses, which are like something addictive and that when you have them once... There is no way to get away from them.

Now tell me something about yourself, because I only know that that is who you are, and that you work in real estate, but I would like to know about your parents and your other family. I will give you a brief summary of my life: I was born in Honduras, my parents and siblings live there, I studied until my Bachelor's degree and due to lack of opportunities I had to emigrate, and by good luck and having found a good boss in my previous job, I got my residence through work, and after studying what I do now I said goodbye to my boss, but not before having fulfilled a commitment we had made and here you have me trying to be better every day, in what I know how to do. I don't miss the opportunity to learn things, I like computers and I read a lot of books to improve my knowledge, apart from keeping my mind busy with positive things. I have my dreams of starting a family, of raising children and having a life full of joy, and of growing old with my beloved wife.

She had remained as if petrified, staring at me and without saying a single word, she was as if hypnotized, as if she had been enchanted by an Indian cobra charmer, but I had to wake her up from her emotional state to continue the dialogue on another level. Now I want to ask you if you want us to get married, and tell me how long it seems appropriate for you and also if you like the idea of having children. Of course I like the idea of having children after getting married, but we have to give ourselves time to enjoy our youth and many things that would not be the same after having them, we also have to get to know each other a little better, since our relationship is very young. . I had not studied psychology, but I got the idea immediately, it seemed that he had a phobia of the idea of having a commitment when procreating children, that he was more interested in the idea of enjoying life, so I no longer insisted on the topic. and I chose to be a little more superficial, like she was being.

I made a mental effort to radically change my mind and went straight to action, which in short I believed was what interested her the most, and I took her hands and kissed them, and I told her: let's not rush everything It is at the right time, neither before nor after, and standing up from my seat I approached her slowly, without taking my eyes off her, so that with her psychoanalysis she would know that I wanted to possess her and that it was serious, and that no matter how much she If I resisted, I couldn't escape from me. And I gently lifted her from her seat, and I hugged her firmly but tenderly, and I began to kiss her passionately, and when she was reciprocated, my kisses became wild, full of burning passion and morbid desires, which forced us to walk towards the bedroom, without detach our lips that seemed glued by the strongest of glues.

This time I did have the trouble to remove the clothes one by one, which deprived me of the immense pleasure of delighting in the observation of her beautiful body, which caused my ravished mind to enter into burning desires to possess her immediately and I had to possess her in form. overwhelming, without allowing her time to think about what was happening, just having time to feel the swing of my excited body that wanted to give her all the manhood I had just for her. And we were like that for a long period of time, in which we enjoyed the delights of wonderful, tender and passionate sex, but at times wild and maddening, in which we felt the electric shocks that accompanied each of our delicious orgasms.

We were left faint, we were like soulless bodies, lying as long as we were, but with a smile of satisfaction that could not be denied, we were as if charged with static electricity, that just touching our bodies produced strange sensations, so we decided that for That day was enough, but without denying the possibility of another meeting for the next day. And we said goodbye with a tender kiss, which seemed like a caricature of the ones we had given each other previously.

After he had left, I went into the bathroom, took a shower with very hot water and went to sleep. I had to regain my strength for the next day of work. I had understood that ours was a sexual attraction and that I didn't know how long it would last, so So I stopped getting my hopes up and decided to enjoy it while it lasted... or maybe I was wrong and it ended in something different, but those thoughts had made me remember that I had a pending commitment, the commitment to find Delilah, for which away, if only to know that he didn't love her anymore... the day he found her.

Once again, after leaving work, I headed to the streets to do my route that I hadn't practiced in a while, and which gave me a little peace in my soul knowing that I was still doing my best to decipher the complexes that confused my mind. As always, I had not been successful in my company, so a little frustrated I returned home to continue with the routine. I had just arrived when I received a call from Rosaura. Her voice sounded very broken and she asked me to come see her. to give him that last satisfaction before dying, so I promised to arrive as soon as possible.

The next day I asked my boss for permission, who did not hesitate to give it to me and after calling Jessica and telling her about my need to travel, he wished me a safe trip and a quick return. With one of my friends I got the ticket for the same day, so I left around midnight, I would arrive in the morning and probably be in Ceiba at noon.  It was only fair that I went to see her when I needed it most, she had given me part of her life and a lot of the knowledge that now had me in a pretty good place, plus maybe she had saved me from a different life if I hadn't had someone to guide me. in my younger years.

As I had planned, I arrived at my destination around noon, I immediately took a taxi that took me directly to Rosaura's house, upon seeing me, the boys who had recognized me immediately took me inside the house where I was. With her mother prostrate, I approached her and timidly asked, How do you feel? She answered weakly: not very well, the Doctor diagnosed me with uterine cancer and it is already advanced, so my days are probably about to end, but I wanted to see you one last time to tell you what I feel, we were alone because of what she kept saying; You were always the great love of my life, I loved you and I love you like no one else I have been able to love and your absence only made me love you more, idolize you as a special being, and I appreciate all the help you have given me, But I thank you more for the time you shared by my side and for all the caresses and tenderness that you knew how to give me during the years you dedicated to me...now I can die peacefully because I know that you fulfilled my last wish, and that I will die with your image in my thoughts waiting for you to accompany me throughout eternity.

I felt enormous sadness, it made me want to cry, to scream in order to express my anguish at seeing my mentor, my friend, my lover and protector, my adoptive mother on her deathbed because she took care of me with care. same care as if I had been his son, I felt angry with destiny that insists on causing the saddest endings, on frustrating the desire to live when one is still young, to realize the most expensive desires for happiness and triumph, but so It is ruthless destiny and we cannot do more than accept its mockery and intransigence. However, I asked to speak to another doctor, in order to have a second opinion, however it coincided with the first diagnosis, and there was nothing left to do but wait for what followed.

At my request, she was transferred to the hospital, where she was cared for very well until the day she passed away to a better life... eternal life. I had covered the funeral expenses and I was with my family who attended the funeral and I had the opportunity to see my parents who were in good health. After finishing the funeral honors, I said goodbye to my family, to the boys whom I advised and I promised my help so that they could finish their studies and I began my return to my new homeland.

Ten days had passed but it seemed like it had been yesterday, as if everything had been a dream, I wish it had been that way. Life is made up of different kinds of situations, happy passages, love, sadness, sex, it is a mosaic of situations that make it interesting because you never know what the next scenario will be, but I expected it to be something happier, although not I had the mood for nothing out of the ordinary. I had called my girlfriend when I arrived at the airport, so she asked me to wait for her to pick me up. Moments later she arrived and in her car the condolences began, because I told her that she had been a very important person in my life. . After arriving at my house she tried to be affectionate, but I wasn't up for those things, so after a brotherly kiss she said goodbye, promising to call me the next day.

It was the weekend, so I dedicated myself to resting and tidying up my house, as well as putting everything in order for the next week of work. On Sunday morning Jessica appeared with a succulent breakfast prepared by her, I was surprised to know that she had made it but I was satisfied to know that she had the skills of a housewife. We ate and watched a variety show on television, so my mind entered another stage, and momentarily forgetting about the tragic events we dedicated ourselves to kissing and caressing each other timidly. But the beast that had been in recess for a few days wanted to make its triumphant appearance and did not hesitate to come out of its lethargy and take on its battle form and began its challenge in front of its opponent who also wanted to enter the battle.

And Troy began to burn, the Trojan horse had been the delicious breakfast and the invading army had been the instincts that were unleashed successively, it was a bloody battle in which we showed off our overwhelming fury and the impetus of our youth, which gave unleashed the entire repertoire of all-out attacks, which ended when the two of us, already tired and exhausted, asked for peace, if at least for that day, and after enjoying all the attributes of it to the fullest, we had to say see you tomorrow or until ASAP.

After Jessica left, my regret came to mind for not respecting the mourning I had to keep for Rosaura, and also for the respect I owed to the memory of Dalila, and I began to feel a little confused, to think that I had no right to love, at least until a reasonable amount of time had passed, and it was then that it occurred to me that we should talk to Jessica, that we should set a time limit for our relationship, in consideration of the women who had been part of my life and I also decided to tell him about my relationship with Dalila, although without telling him what had been a reason for my emotional imbalance, which had not yet fully healed.

After asking him to come to my house, he told me that he would arrive until Saturday because he had classes and he didn't want to miss them, because the exams were approaching and he had to stay up to date. And Saturday arrived and when she showed up in the morning I had no choice but to postpone the talk, she was so beautiful with her summer dress of various colors on a yellow background, and with her smile radiant with joy, in addition to another of her prepared meals. with his little hands.  I didn't have the courage to ruin his day, he was so happy that I didn't want to be the reason that his happiness turned into another feeling and that he suffered because of me, so after giving me a passionate kiss and inviting me to enjoy the culinary delights, we went to the dining room where he prepared to serve the table at the same time he asked me: what did you want to tell me? I had to lie, and I invented a white lie to avoid messing things up, and we ate and looked at each other like two lovers.

After eating we didn't spend time watching a movie on television, and while she was absorbed in the movie, I gave myself a little time to meditate, and it was then that I reasoned: Rosaura gave me what she could give me, but she no longer belonged to this world, she was gone and we had to let her rest. As for Dalila, although I was the one who pushed her to make that decision, I couldn't turn back time and try to make it happen.

different, so I thought the best thing was to try to be happy with Jessica and forget everything that was a sad and sometimes bitter past, and we would try to be happy at whatever cost.

And morbidity began to take over my mind when I saw her dress above her knees given the position when she was sitting, and I began to touch her delicate skin with caresses that were more than provocative, wait, I want to finish watching the movie, he said, but the film was unnecessary, the heat of my caresses and the fire of my kisses, the malice of my caresses on his most sensitive parts... and he succumbed, he couldn't take it anymore and ended up giving up everything, to correspond to my wishes with her desires, to begin a maelstrom of feelings that were complemented by action, with the movement of our bodies seeking each other to trigger a series of vibrant orgasms, which transported us to unknown dimensions in which there was only room for two.

And there we were, we had the first orgasm on the sofa, then we threw ourselves on the carpet because we needed space to give free rein to our sexual madness, our desire to merge body and soul, to waste all our energy and evacuate torrents of virile liquid and feminine liquid, to in this way give proof of our love. I don't know who was more aggressive, but only fatigue was able to separate us and make our bodies seek refuge in peace, which surely would not last for long, but which was a wise resource.

And at the end of a wonderful day, we had to say goodbye and propose to meet the next day when we would have time to go anywhere, that is if we didn't fall into temptation. He arrived very early, this time he also brought me something delicious and after consuming it he asked me to go to the beach to enjoy a delicious sunny day. He had the necessary things in a sports bag and under his shorts and a beach blouse he was already wearing wearing her tiny swimsuit, when we arrived we spread out some large towels to sunbathe and she asked me to apply her sunscreen, it was a unique sight because dressed in her swimsuit the last thing she wanted was to lie in the sun, on the contrary they wanted to be lying on the carpet in my house. But we also had to enjoy the delights of nature, and remembering my younger years back in my homeland, we enjoyed a beautiful day at the beach.

We had sunbathed, but we had also swam a little in the cold waters of the Pacific Ocean, and we filled ourselves with sand, and when we got home we decided to take a bath to remove the salt and sand stuck to our bodies. "I went first," she said and headed to the bathroom, "it's okay," I said and let her pass, but my curiosity had not forgotten when I applied the sunscreen, so pretending to take something from the bathroom, I approached to watch her when she took off naked. the sand and salt from the body, and feigning a disinterested attitude I asked him: do you want me to help you remove the one from your back? And she agreed, when I got into the tub with her inside I had to take off the clothes I was wearing leaving us both naked, I couldn't contain my instinct and before I realized I was already hugging and kissing her, and with my sex burning with the desire to possess her in any way possible.

I had never experienced making love in the bathtub before, but it was a very pleasant experience, because if we sweated we didn't realize it because the water was responsible for keeping us clean and cool, although in the same way we were exhausted and sleepy, so we had what to say: until next week. She left but she left me with a pleasant memory. I would think about her, about her physical qualities, and about the hotness of her sex that filled me with delight in every sense of the word, about the tenderness of her caresses but also about the offensiveness. which was at the time of their loving reciprocity. It seemed that we were on the right track, we had been like-minded in every way and I wanted everything to end at the altar.

And to continue with the routine, work and everything else, but there was a question inside me that I hoped would find a solution very soon, it was very nice to be surprised from time to time by the presence of my girlfriend, apart from having sexual encounters but for That was not enough for me, because my dream was to get married and have a family, raise children and establish my own offspring. That day it occurred to me to ask Jessica if she wanted to marry me and propose a date so I could ask her parents for her hand, so I called her to ask her when we could see each other.

As always, he answered that it would be Saturday, so I waited until that day with the idea of giving him a surprise. I had gone to a reputable jewelry store and bought a beautiful engagement ring, a six-mm princess-cut wide-arm solitaire in white gold that I hoped would be to her liking, the price was not transcendental, since she deserved that and more. So I was waiting until Saturday, with the anxiety and nervousness of a teenager.

As always he surprised me early on Saturday morning, he arrived like Little Red Riding Hood, with his basket of food to satisfy the big bad wolf's appetite, hello my love he said and giving me a tender good morning kiss he went to the dining room table to place the food, and she asked me to prepare the coffee while she was doing that, which turned out very delicious, she argued, and we dedicated ourselves to delighting in the delicious breakfast that was getting better and better.

After the sumptuous meal we headed to the living room to watch some television, I left her entertained while I washed my mouth and went to the bedroom to pick up the ring that came in a cute little blue box, and I also had a beautiful red rose in the part of the vegetables from the refrigerator, which I brought at the same time, I stood in front of her and getting on my knees asked her to agree to marry me and I gave her the rose with one hand and with the other I placed the ring with the open box in front of her. his eyes. She uttered a loud exclamation of astonishment and with teary eyes she told me that yes, her dream had been to get married in white in a church full of flowers, and that it was even better with a man so handsome and virile, as well as hardworking. After kissing me for a long time he separated from me and said: I have to call my mother to tell her, I can't believe it!

That same afternoon and after telling them about my visit by phone, we went to their house (which I had sold to them) and there together with their parents, I asked for their authorization to set a date for our union. They were very surprised to find out who I was, but they did not resist, because they knew that she was already of age and that what we were doing was informing them of our intentions and to fill certain social parameters. And making it a little exciting, they set a one-year deadline for said marriage.

Well, now our relationship already had the approval of her parents, and our job would be to start planning ahead of time and enjoy our love in everything that being single allowed us, so she suggested that we go to my house that very soon it would be hers too and enjoy a celebratory evening. Before leaving her house she stopped by her bedroom to bring some things, and after arriving at mine she went into the bathroom, from which she came out dressed in a nice dressing gown and some casual sandals. She looked so homely and while she was preparing something in the kitchen I approached her from behind, when I hugged her I instantly felt that she was not wearing any underwear, which awakened my desire to possess her, so taking her waist with my hands I began to kiss her neck , then I raised my hands to place them on her large and solid breasts, she could not stand my insinuating caresses and she turned to face each other and offered me her delicious lips that joined mine in a passionate kiss.

I had lifted her up in suspense and transported her to my bedroom where I removed her light robe that was between her body and mine, and I began to kiss her with more intensity and we then fell into a constant and maddening back and forth, rhythmic and ardent that woke her up again. our wildest instincts, which gave us immense satisfaction in a constant succession of orgasms. It was a constant waste of energy, something that seemed like an addiction because as soon as we recovered from fatigue, the desire to possess ourselves awoke again and we were like that for incalculable periods of time, but it made us immensely happy.

And I thought that this was the remedy I had been waiting for to forget about Dalila, because I hardly remembered her anymore and I didn't feel guilty about my actions either, and the time I had to look for her I began to use it to educate myself to the maximum, there was no book that would escape my desire to soak my mind in knowledge, to enrich my knowledge in all fields, to be able to function in any field in which I had the opportunity to talk or get advice for any eventuality, but in particular I was preparing myself so that My children will have true support as they begin their path through life.

I was super excited to think that in just a year I would no longer be alone, that I would no longer spend the nights talking to myself, that I would have someone to share my sorrows and my joys with, I could make any comment and have a response to it, I wouldn't have to eat. alone or feeling bored on rainy afternoons or on oppressively hot days. The sun had come into my life, the light that would dispel the darkness of my loneliness, the warm body that would give me its energy to be happy, giving me its tenderness and womanly charms, giving me the opportunity to fulfill myself as a husband and as a father. .

There were a whole host of reasons to feel happy, there were so many that I didn't know which ones were most important, although in my way of thinking I knew that all the reasons were important in themselves, no matter the order in which they were placed, I knew that happiness was knocking on the doors of my life and I couldn't stop receiving it now that destiny had finally decided to make amends for all the damage it had decided to do to me. And I asked the mocking destiny; That this time he was not going to be treacherous and give me a little happiness and then give me mouthfuls of bitterness, I asked him to be fair and repay me for all the suffering he had given me with Delilah's love.

And I woke up from my deep thinking, and I continued contemplating my beloved and I filled my thoughts with her figure and my sense of smell with her aroma, to remember her as I looked at her at that moment when she was completely mine. And as if he heard my thoughts, he asked me: do you think that romance will be lost when we get married?, and I answered: it will not end while our love and our instincts are active, and on the contrary, our union will be strengthened upon the arrival of our offspring. I could see that the expression of doubt appeared on his face, as if pronouncing the word offspring would erase part of the charm of our relationship, as if offspring would take away what was magical and exciting about our love.

I didn't want to erase from my mind everything beautiful about our relationship in the face of a superficial comment, and I tried to find a way for our meeting to end in the best way. So I asked him what plans he had for the following week, so he assured me that it would be an exhausting week, since he would be taking exams to finish his degree and he could then begin to take advantage of so many hours of study. She said goodbye somewhat worried, as if the idea of marriage had shocked her, and promised that she would call me the next day. I was also worried when I thought that perhaps I had asked for marriage too soon, but with time things would become clearer, now I had to think about selling more houses and growing financially for what was foreseen in the future.

I had not studied psychology, but I had a very deep use of common sense and logic, so I knew that something was not right, because the next day when I had the opportunity to speak on the phone with Jessica, I noticed a restlessness in her voice, It was as if something was bothering her and she didn't have the courage to say it or discuss it, so I, who had always been very clear, motivated her to tell me what was happening to her. She didn't say it, but she promised me that on Saturday we were going to talk about certain things that were important for us to clarify, so I had no choice but to wait, and so the week went by without us talking about it.

Saturday arrived and as usual he showed up early in the morning with breakfast, it seemed as if everything was fine, but deep down in our relationship there was a vibe that predicted that a storm was coming; It was like the omen that there was going to be a confrontation of incalculable magnitude. I didn't want to broach the subject, as I considered it inappropriate, but after we had eaten and headed towards the sofa, he looked at me as if wanting to know my state of mind so he could start the dialogue. And I didn't make her wait any longer and asked what the unrest was and that she shouldn't be shy about telling me whatever it was, that after all we were civilized and broad-minded people.

Look, it began, I know that you have a slightly different concept of life because you come from a different culture, but I was raised in a more liberal society and therefore, despite believing in love, I have a different perspective on marriage, for me. Marriage is about growing in different ways and enjoying a healthy relationship and sharing in all aspects, family, social, etc. but I also want to enjoy life in terms of walking, knowing, growing in my profession and having the means to live comfortably in my old age, but I do not want to spoil my figure through pregnancies, grow old by breastfeeding children and enslaving myself. because they have to be taken care of all the time, that's not for me. So reconsider your request for marriage, and if you think that I am not the wife that suits you, even if it hurts me, I will be willing to consider the engagement broken.

I felt that the ground was sinking under my feet, I who always pretended to have control of the situation felt that I could not control anything, I who believed that destiny had changed its aberration towards me I realized that this was not the case, and that it continued determined to cause me harm, to ruin all the dreams I had made for myself. But gathering courage and not giving up in the face of merciless fate, I tried to minimize things and assured her that I agreed with what she considered was best for her and our union and pretending that I was not upset I pulled her towards me and I kissed her like I always did.

Well, it starts with something, and as marriages do, we ended our differences on the throne of Aphrodite, we wanted to forget our differences by paying tribute to the goddess of love and we began the ritual that would be dedicated in her honor. I had undressed her and was contemplating her body, which was like an aphrodisiac that enervated my instincts and altered my emotions, which unleashed a burning passion that made me possess her for endless moments, full of unbridled lust that ended in uncontrollable death rattles of pleasure, The most delicious orgasms were consummated one by one, and we were almost dead, with satisfaction and exhaustion.

She would give time to time, perhaps in the future her maternal instinct would awaken and she would decide to have children, and in the meantime we would enjoy our love and our sexual appetite and other pleasures of life, anyway we were young and we had everything time ahead, and at least I was not giving pleasure to the inexorable destiny that was always against me. So the only thing we could do was; enjoy and wait for the end of the year that had been set as a limit to arrive.

I don't know, but even though Jessica was a woman who met all expectations, I began to feel that our relationship had already focused specifically on sex, and that after having our encounters it seemed that there was no other incentive to feel loved, because so I suggested that we give ourselves time so that we would know what was really happening. She had also realized the situation and agreed with me, so we suggested not seeing each other for at least a month to see what reaction each of us would have.

Bad thing, because as we grew apart, the apathy of both of us worsened, and I only remembered her when the monster wanted to make his appearance, so I understood that our thing had come to an end, but nevertheless I called her to find out what It happened to her. She didn't answer the first two calls, but as always the third is the charm, so after greeting her I asked her if it would be possible for us to meet and that it would be best if we met in neutral territory, to be able to better define our feelings, she accepted. and we agreed to meet at the place where we had our first romantic meetings.

He arrived at the place where we had had dinner and had the first bottle of wine, we ordered the same thing and taking my hands he asked me: what did we not do well to be in this situation? I didn't know what to say, but I assumed that our attraction had been superficial and that is why it did not stand the test of time, but I suggested that we try one more time and after dinner and drinking the bottle of wine, perhaps the fumes of alcohol motivated us to head towards my house where we arrived. with morbidity at its maximum expression.

However, I wanted to give him a night that would be difficult for him to forget in case it was his last, so I used tactics from when I had to satisfy women versed in sex (sexservants) and I began my art of satisfying, melting icebergs. of ice with the burning of my experience, poor me who always wanted to enjoy the same as her, now what I wanted was for her to go crazy with pleasure, to convince herself that no one else could make her happy and that when being with someone else she would repeat my name and wishing that I was the one who was with her, I had transformed myself into a mean, vile being and all the similar names, without knowing why, what I wanted was to avenge my frustration of having to leave her for the reason of not wanting to give me children and preferring forget our commitment. I wanted to punish her for destroying my illusions, for making me build castles in the air and now leaving me as a village bride, dressed and fussy.

I felt like she had become a puppet and I was pleased to play with her. I felt sorry for her when she was panting, as if she wanted to say no more, but her pride made her contain that impulse and she continued to suffer with the succession of orgasms, which began to become more intense. like a martyrdom for his nervous system that was about to collapse, he was sweating profusely and it seemed that his eyes were turning completely white, without pupils and exorbitant, that I began to feel afraid that he might fade away, so I became human for a few moments… I stopped making her suffer and stopped any action that could have fatal consequences. She almost succumbed, because seeing her in such a bad state I had to run to the refrigerator to bring her water to drink and revive her by throwing some on her face, how cruel and mean I had been to the poor young woman, so I promised myself not to. have any relationship with her again.

He was unconscious for a long time, until he weakly got up from the bed and looking at me with fear he said: did you want to kill me or did you just want to leave your mark on me, so that I can't forget you? I could only answer: I promise you that It will not happen again. Don't worry, I liked it but I think it's something very strong for me, tell me why were you different this time? I didn't have a proper response, I could only say; I went too far and that's all, but I think I did wrong, I'm sorry. I felt confused and just wanted him to leave, I wanted to be alone so I could put my thoughts in order and analyze what it was that I really wanted.

I thought later when I was alone that: what I had looked for in women other than Dalila had been sex, that everything I believed to be love was only the desire to find someone who was compatible with my animal instinct, that what I I was more interested in satisfying myself and sexual desires and nothing more. So I felt frustrated, defeated and regretted my actions, but I made a promise to myself to be different in the future and I would try to be a normal man, not to abuse my ability to destroy any woman with the super specialness of me. sexual power.

The next day I called Jessica and asked her to forgive me for my wild and irrational way of treating a woman and I assured her that I didn't want to hurt her again, to end our engagement, and that from now on we would just be friends. if she wanted it, but that she was in no way obligated to have any relationship with me. She answered: then your words and your promises were a lie? All your caresses and flattering phrases were to possess me? I could only tell her; everything was true until you decided to break my heart by denying me the privilege of being a father, only because of your obsession with maintaining a beautiful body, forgetting how important children are for a marriage, but nevertheless maybe in the future it will wake up again the sentimental attraction between us, do you want us to give each other a couple of months of time? She replied that it was fine with her and that we would keep in touch and see what happened.

I followed my routine, work hard and store wealth, soak my mind and strengthen my body, and I no longer thought about any woman, I wanted to give myself time to detoxify my mind and start fresh in the future. The woman who had occupied my mind and my heart for so long was becoming a sweet memory and the feelings of guilt that tormented me were turning into resignation and forgetfulness. I had decided to wait until true love appeared knocking on my heartstrings and I could then begin a relationship based on nothing but love. So when Jessica called I tried not to answer or if she did I would ask her to call later claiming to be very busy or with a client.

The two-month deadline passed and the following Saturday; She appeared as she had done for many Saturdays, with her basket of delicious food and her cheerful smile that brightened my morning. I was very happy to see her because she had already been like a hermit for some time, lonely and without the female presence. I greeted her with the attention that characterized me when I acted normally, and I actually felt great joy because I considered her a good friend. Come in, I told him, I'm very happy to see you and you didn't have to bother bringing anything, you know that your presence is more than enough, but anyway I'll prepare the coffee that I know you like. She looked so beautiful that I wanted to kiss her, but like me she had refrained from doing so, but she set the table with the same joy and served the food that we began to consume willingly, as we were very close she spread her hands. hands to take one of mine and told me: it makes me very happy to see you again and I don't hold any resentment for what you told me, besides I still love you the same as always and I ask that we try to start with new vigor, do you think? ?

I couldn't resist the temptation to see her so happy, freshly bathed and with that delicious aroma of her perfume, her finely outlined red lips and her loose hair, all clad in a colorful dress in pastel tones that served as a frame for her natural beauty. We had finished the food and after collecting the dishes we sat on the sofa, but not before rinsing our mouths and getting ready to watch television. The daring neckline revealed the charms of her massive breasts, which had made my mind begin to plot morbid desires, I wanted to concentrate on ignoring them, but she helped prevent that from happening, she approached me with her lips half open. , inducing me to kiss her and begin to delight in the nectar of her mouth, I could not stop my hands that automatically began to travel over her body, to delight in traveling through her massive curves that shook my entire being, but this time I wanted us both to enjoy and we would suffer the electric shocks of multiple orgasms.

This time it was a passionate and delicate delivery, this time the master insisted on seducing her sweetly, with mischief but without malice, with elegance and showing off a delicate language, which made her give herself body and soul, and sigh in her heart. each lilting movement that unnerved her more and more. Time passed and we were not able to finish so much delight, because we barely stopped for a few minutes and we already wanted to start again with our tireless and rhythmic love, to mix our liquids that flowed in a torrent of inexhaustible fury.

It had gotten dark without us realizing it, because when we were in our idyll we forgot everything that was around us, but we returned to reality because we already needed to replenish fluids and eat something to replace a little of the lost energy. So we urged her to get dressed, but not before taking a stimulating shower that revived us a little, and we headed to a nice restaurant to celebrate reconciliation.

After a delicious dinner accompanied by a delicious Chardonnay, we returned to my house so she could pick up her car to go home, however it seemed that the break of more than two months kept her still wanting to have a little more delicious sex, and without asking anything he told me that we should watch a little television and then we would go to sleep. Intrigued, I asked, are you sure? And I received a response of "sure yes!"

Well, maybe the isolation had made her reconsider and have a different idea of what she wanted from life, or maybe she just wanted us to enjoy being single for the moment, whatever it was we were going to enjoy it to the fullest and tomorrow we would see what the rest. While we were watching a show on television, I stopped to think about how good she was in every way, except for her phobia of having children, so I thought that maybe she was right and that we could be happy even without them, so it occurred to me that we were going to continue with our relationship despite everything and that we would enjoy it day by day without thinking about anything other than our happiness.

And we continued to see each other every Saturday and Sunday, and during the rest of the week we only communicated by phone. She had graduated as a psychologist and was working in a prestigious clinic in Beverly Hills. Her dealings with people of different cultural and economic levels made her She began to become a little vain, her discrimination towards people of humble status was felt and that began to worry me and to feel a certain misgiving again, which meant that we began to distance ourselves even without intending to and that she found any pretext to delay our meetings.

Things always fall by their own weight, and without saying anything we stopped seeing each other and not even phone calls connected us anymore, the charm had been broken and this time it was definitive, because one Saturday there was a knock at the door and unconsciously I I imagined it was her, but what would be my surprise when I saw her sister standing in front of me, I invited her to come in and asked her what the reason for her visit was, to which she replied that she was sorry for the reason for her visit, but that his sister asked him to bring back the engagement ring that I had given her, and that he did not do it personally for fear of falling for my charms again.

# CHAPTER SEVEN

She had not noticed how pretty her younger sister Elena was, she was the same height as her and had almost all of her attributes as well, with the difference that her gaze was more serene and passionate and that her eyes were light brown and her Darker hair, she also had a larger bust as well as her buttocks that were rounder and bulkier, her voice was sweet and gentle, which gave her that touch of elegance. After receiving the ring and putting it on the coffee table I thanked her for the message and asked her if she would like to have something to drink, she asked me if I had pure water since she was trying to lose weight, of course I had nothing to lose since I had an enviable body, so I flattered her and told her what I thought.

She looked at me analytically and told me: I think I know the reason why my sister went crazy for you, and I think she really is crazy to give up a man like you, but tell me, is it true that you kiss so delicious? Well, my Sister says your kisses are maddening. I didn't have to answer, I just blushed and tried to evade the topic, but she insisted by saying: sin accuses you and that's why you don't say anything, but since I won't return to this house, let me try just one of those dreamy, approaching kisses. She grabbed me by the neck and pulling me towards her, she placed her lips on mine, in a very daring way and sucked my lips with an innocent, but at the same time seductive kiss.

I didn't want to touch her body and that was the reason she had pulled me, or maybe it was because deep down I felt a certain attraction to being so beautiful and beautiful, I didn't want to think, so I did what my instinct told me. I suggested…and taking her by the waist I pressed her against my body and began to kiss her as one kisses a girlfriend on the first date, tenderly and softly and trying to send her all the energy in each suction of lips and the rose of the tongues that They were soaked in the delicious nectar of his mouth. And we stayed like that for a long time, as if wanting time to stop so as not to separate us and enjoy the exquisiteness of that long kiss. Suddenly she separated and after a long sigh she looked into my eyes, as if wanting to see through them into the interior of my soul and know what I was feeling at that moment, to scrutinize in my thoughts what I felt for her.

She looked at my anxiety, she could see my excitement and it was then that I could see a hint of malice in her, it was then that she approached me more suggestively and offered me her lips again, but this time in a more exciting way, then it was that She transformed into a tigress who wanted to devour her prey, to eat her alive kiss by kiss. For a moment I had the necessary lucidity and I separated her from my side and told her: we can't do that, you are very young and you are her sister, it is crazy, but she answered me: I am also a woman and I feel the same as her, I am I am of legal age and I want to be yours, whoever likes it. She was very convincing and while we were there kissing, she began to remove herself, one by one, the clothes that served as a hindrance to letting herself be possessed by someone she had desired since the first time she met me.

Only when I saw her beautiful naked body could I fully appreciate how desirable she was, and getting rid of my clothes at the speed of light, I threw myself into her arms, to take the honey of what seemed crazy to me, but was worth the money. shame to go crazy It was a delight to caress the softness of her mons pubis, to run my hands over her long legs until I reached her bulging and smooth buttocks from behind, to squeeze her massive breasts with their tiny nipples and caress them with my tongue and listen to her moans that demanded be possessed I had already waited long enough, I was already quite excited so penetrating her was the next step, it was a slow, gentle and unhurried penetration, we had to enjoy it to its fullest and then begin the back and forth that produced the most unspeakable sensations in us.

She moaned, she screamed, she clung to me and buried her nails in my back, she was a beast in heat and I had to express what I felt, to shout from the rooftops that I was immensely happy, and after endless orgasms, we were exhausted, lying side by side trying to suck the air that our lungs were missing. And we stayed like that for a long time, trying to regain strength to be able to speak and tell each other how much we enjoyed it. After what happened, it seemed that she had been embarrassed and covering her face she said to me: Forgive me, but my sister talked to me so much about you that without wanting to, I fell in love and I wished with all my soul that you would notice me and make me yours so that I would know. what it felt like to be loved by a real man. I know that I did not offer you my virginity because I lost it with my first boyfriend, but I did not feel anything since he only wanted to satisfy himself without thinking that I also deserved to be satisfied, and since then I had not had sex again, until today when I found out what which is to be loved and satisfied in its entirety.

I hope that you are not going to leave me excited as happened with my sister, because I will do everything possible so that our love grows and regenerates every day, so that it is always active and yearning. He was anticipating my words, because as soon as I could react I told him: this does not have to be repeated, this is crazy that should not have happened and I ask you to reason and think about the damage that having sex without contraceptive protection can cause you. Can you imagine what your parents would say if they knew and what they would think of me? He answered me: don't worry, I know how to take care of myself and my parents would accept any decision I make, since I am already of age and I support myself, so it would be the same for me to live with them than to live alone or with you, but it would be better if at your side I urged her to leave and suggested that she let me think about it, that she call me in a couple of days to think about what to do, she left very excited, and promised to wait.

I woke up on Sunday very thoughtful, I didn't know what to do because I thought she was too cute for me to get her excited and then forget about her, but it also occurred to me that we could be happy and formalize a home, what a dilemma! But I would try to find a way to solve it during the week, I felt guilty for not being able to avoid it and letting us get tangled up in that situation, but there was no way it was done and now I had to find a solution. Maybe there was no need to think too much, after all she was a single woman just like I was single, so it didn't hurt to try a relationship that could last longer than you might think.

I started the work week, now with new enthusiasm and happy that she was such an ardent and expressive woman, quite liberal for her young age and with the desire to start a long-lasting relationship, but the dilemma was, what would we say to her family? and his sister the day they found out?, in the course of my short existence I had learned not to worry about the day I had not yet seen, so I would take the risk of continuing the relationship and trying to make everything go well.

On Tuesday afternoon I received her call, she asked me how I was feeling and that when I wanted to meet, she worked part-time in a dental clinic as a secretary and in the afternoons she went to school, so she had a little more time so we could see each other during the week. So I told him that I was home most of the time after work and that he could come whenever he wanted. And it began to arrive daily and devour me to the point of exhaustion, so that what seemed to me to be the beginning of a loving relationship had become the most ruthless war of the sexes. It was delicious, I won't deny it, but it turns out that a relationship in which sex was the main thing was overwhelming, I wanted to put love before any other feeling, but in her immaturity she thought that having sex every day was true love.

We were like this for eight or nine weeks, in which we only stopped having sex on her period days, but I was already getting upset because as soon as she saw us she would tell me: I love you, and she would start to provoke our meeting, so that day I told him: I want you not to get angry with what I am going to tell you, but I think you are confusing what love is, love is a set of feelings, it is being able to share a talk, have an afternoon of meditation on the beach or in somewhere relaxing, is sharing dreams and hopes and making plans for the future, and not just going to bed and having sex and then saying see you later, I suggest we change our routine and get to know each other better in the deepest aspects, do you think?

It seemed like I had slapped her in the face, she turned red and had a defiant face, as if trying to get me to take back my words, and then, all angry, she told me: it's never good with you, now I know why my sister left you. and the one who does not understand my love is you, I have intended by giving you my body and my caresses, by giving you my passionate kisses and all my womanly charms, that you would be happy, that you would feel with my delivery how much I love you , but instead you reproach me, how badly you interpret my love!, but I think maybe it's because you don't deserve it, I'd better go and if you think differently, call me.

I felt confused, I didn't know how to react and I just let her go, I didn't understand what I did wrong and I preferred to take my time to analyze my attitude, and ask for forgiveness if necessary or let her return on her own. The pillow is always the best advisor, so I waited until I went to sleep to ask her for advice, I was meditating on my words and hers, in reality that was my problem, that's why all my relationships had failed, that's why Dalila had also left, and I understood that deep down I was the same as Elena, because I had always put sex before my true feelings. I believed that deep down I had some complex that didn't let me see beyond what I now wanted me to see. Elena will look.

And the next morning I called her to ask her to forgive me for my attitude, and I asked her to meet that night so I could explain my fears and my complexes. I knew beforehand that the reason for my way of being was because due to my precocity my entire relationship with women revolved around sex and my platonic love, because in my immaturity I thought I could love everyone I had. sex, and I thought that she was having a similar problem, because in her immaturity and her failure with her first boyfriend she had suffered some small trauma, which made her value sex as true love.

Night came and we had a reunion, but before any action I asked him to listen to me; Elena, I want you to listen to me carefully since I don't want you to misinterpret my words, my affection for you has been taking a different course than what my dream is, I want to love you and feel loved, not necessarily while being in bed making love, I want That we walk hand in hand anddaydreamabout more beautiful things, that when we are not together you think of me and miss me for my qualities as a human being and not as a sex machine, sex is magical and delicious but only It must be the complement of love, so that it remains beautiful all the time, but if we put it as a basis, surely the day we can't do it neither of us will feel anything, one for the other and vice versa.

She had been silent, listening and staring at me without even blinking, but when I finished speaking she said: now you will listen to me, when I met you I was emotionally impacted by your physical appearance, in addition to your good manners in treating people, and I felt what They call it love at first sight, but to my luck, bad or good, my sister had more trouble to get ahead of me and in that way she was your girlfriend or lover, but as time went by I started to want to be with you in bed, because of the experiences that my sister half told me, because she couldn't be too explicit, but that I guessed from her passion when she told me, and I was jealous of you knowing that she was enjoying what I had not found because I was slow. But now that you have opened my eyes, I will try to enjoy your love in all the forms that exist and that I will discover along the way of our relationship.

I felt extremely moved when I heard her words, and in response I embraced her in my arms and kissed her with the sweetness that my soul could express, and then we fell into a trance of sublime sex, where we made our souls vibrate, at the same time that Our bodies were satiated to the maximum, being burned in the last and delirious orgasm. When she said goodbye, she asked me if I wanted to go to a friend's birthday party the following Saturday. I replied that I would be delighted and asked how I could dress and she replied: either way you'll look good, until then!

The day of the party arrived and we were transported in my car, which by then was already a recent model and somewhat elegant, after arriving he introduced me as his friend to some friends, and we were talking with them when Jessica suddenly appeared , who upon seeing us together was surprised and, leaving the man who was accompanying her, approached us, hello, I said hello, but I did not receive a response to my greeting, on the contrary, he attacked me with questions without caring that others heard what he said. What do you want now with my sister? Wasn't it enough for you to have me as your sex toy? Do you want to do the same with my sister? Although she had lowered her voice, there would be no shortage of people listening to her comments, so I discreetly asked Elena to leave and told Jessica that if she wanted to discuss the topic she already knew where to find me.

I couldn't understand how a person with so much knowledge and social skills could behave in that way, although maybe she did know and I thought it was jealousy, protection of her younger sister and frustration at not being the one who was fulfilling herself, but It didn't justify her actions and we returned home with Elena, who was also a little uncomfortable by her sister's attitude. Let's have coffee and watch a movie on TV, I suggested, maybe then we'll forget about the incident.

We were sitting there with the cup in our hands, when loud knocks were heard at the door. It was Jessica who, not happy with the scene at the party, had headed to my house with the feeling that she would find us there. I couldn't deny her access. Well anyway there was nothing she could do, plus it was a more discreet place where we could talk, she had left her friend in the car and she faced us both in a threatening manner, but we didn't flinch and let her to talk to.

You are shameless André, just like you Elena, because you know that she is my younger sister and you know that he was my boyfriend and that there were more than kisses and hugs, besides you have no future with someone who is interested in women just for the sake of it. a certain amount of time, and when he gets bored of them he looks for another, but look at you, you are now in my place. Or did you believe his promises of marriage, or his dreams of starting a family and being happy? Tell me André, did you? What did you want was to make fun of me with my sister? Or did you want to tell her the same things that you told me every time you made love to me? Until that moment we had only listened to her, but it was time to answer her, first it was me and I said : In the things of love nothing is written and no one can give an opinion because no one knows the thoughts and feelings of a couple, you and I had our chance and it didn't work out for some reason, don't meddle in our lives now and let us try at least to be happy.

It was Elena's turn who said: sister, I have always respected you and I have never reproached you for anything, but you were the one who pushed me into André's arms, because you knew that I liked him and despite that, whenever you were with him you came telling me about how wonderful he was in bed, and now that I've seen it, I'm not going to lose him for anything in the world, and what he tells me about that will only be between the two of us, so don't interfere in our lives and try to be happy with him. the man who is now part of your life. And he left, but not before threatening to tell his parents what had happened.

I knew that stormy times were coming, I could guess it in Jessica's eyes, but perhaps they would be louder for poor Elena, although before she left I assured her that she could count on me for anything, and if she had to leave her My house would always be with the doors open for her. So she left more certain of what she had to do in case her parents put too much pressure on her, so we said goodbye with a nervous kiss and, strangely enough, we were happy and without having had intimate relations, which proved that sex It only complements love.

I went to sleep but I couldn't fall asleep, I was on the lookout in case Elena suddenly arrived with her personal things after her parents took her out of their house, but I knew that her parents were intelligent people and that they would first try to convince her in case that they judged that what she was doing was wrong, which calmed me down and let me sleep after tossing and turning in bed for a while.

I got up early as usual, picked up the newspaper that bothered me on the weekends and got ready to drink coffee after having taken an invigorating shower. I was pouring my coffee when I heard a knock on the door. It immediately occurred to me that it could be Jessica. , but to my liking it was Elena, who was carrying a box with fast food, but who was still grateful for the intention. After serving it and starting to eat, she began to excitedly tell me what had happened when she got home.

Notice that when I got home, my parents were in the living room waiting for me and with their faces upset, at first I was afraid but when I remembered your support I felt strong and I asked them why they were awake at that hour, my father was the one. who spoke and said: we know that you are with this André and that you have romantic relations with him, even though you know he was engaged to your sister, don't you feel sorry for your attitude?, and added that that was not the way to move from a woman of principles and responsibilities to a decent home. Look dad, with all the respect you deserve, I want you to remember that I am a person of legal age, that I have use of all my faculties and therefore I know how to manage my life and not interfere in that of others, which my sister what she told them is not really something that concerns her and therefore I think they are drowning in a glass of water. So I suggested that they worry about other things that might be more important, instead of correcting what had no reason to be corrected, and saying good night I went to my bedroom to rest, which I really missed.

And we stayed like that for about six months, until we began to feel a certain anger due to the routine, because when we talked or when we went out to the movies the first thing that came up for her to talk was if I liked how we had done it in the morning and If I would like to have a fantasy, or if I liked it more that she was on top taking the initiative, we had tried all the positions in the Kama Sutra, but what didn't make sense was that everything we did and talked about began or ended with sex. , I don't deny that she had all the necessary elements to always desire her, but what drove me crazy was that there was no other topic we could talk about, so I thought that she had some psychological disorder and that perhaps her sister could help her. help, so I thought I would advise her to consult with Jessica to help her with the problem.

That Saturday night when he visited me, I suggested that we go for a walk to the beach and eat at a restaurant that he liked. He immediately replied that we could order something over the phone and thus have more time to enjoy it in bed. I asked myself what How good will I be at doing it? Or is it that I actually have a big one? Well, that didn't matter, but it was at that moment that I suggested that she talk to her sister about it, since it could be that she had a disorder of any nature and who better than her to advise her; He got angry again and told me: if I want to do it all the time it is because I love you and because you are tired you don't feel like doing it with anyone else, which guarantees me that your love is only for me, but I see that it is impossible for You can agree with my ideas, but if you don't like it then let's get married and then I will know that you will always be with me.

I thought that she wouldn't know what would be worse, the illness or the medicine, so I had to tell her that maybe she was right and that we should think about marriage, so very excited she hugged me and kissed me sweetly and asked me to go celebrate. for such a good idea. By coincidence we went to the place where we had gone with Jessica so many times, and as I was listening to the violin with its lilting and melancholic notes, I felt that what he was doing with his sister was not gentlemanly, so embarrassed with myself I decided that that would be the last night that I would be with her, and that I would try by all means to get out of her life so that Elena could find someone who would respect her, since what I did was truly immoral, leaving my sister behind. getting involved with her, I should have avoided that from day one.

After getting home I started my strategy, we had had a few drinks so she was euphoric and hotter than other times, so I thought of giving her the same medicine as her sister, I started by arousing her to the maximum, when she was already asking almost loudly. being possessed, I began with my merciless undulating movement, with my constant and aggressive pushing, so that only she would melt while I only watched her wear and tear, at first she began to enjoy herself but as she satiated her instincts, she began to feel that the joy was fading. transformed into boredom, to feeling that what caused her pleasure became martyrdom, and what gave her delight when penetrating her became something that hurt her, that irritated her by evaporating her liquids that had come out in torrents, no more, No more, she asked piteously, but I didn't listen to her pleas until suddenly, all hysterical, she began to cry and say: what a miserable animal, do you think I'm a machine? Don't you realize that I'm made of flesh and blood? You are insensitive, beast! And since I didn't stop acting, she desperately managed to get away from me and sitting on the bed she started crying and cursing me, I thought I had achieved my goal, I felt meaner with what I had done but I thought I had achieved my goal.

After crying for a long time she got up, and after going to the bathroom she came out again already dressed, she looked at me with uncertainty, as if she didn't know what to say, then her look turned angry and she said: I never believed you were capable of transforming yourself into a monster, you seemed mentally insane, a sadist who enjoys destroying another being, a sexual predator who enjoys watching his victims suffer, I will never forgive you for this and I hope you pay for your infamy. I didn't have words to make her feel better, or they didn't come out of my mouth, because I felt the taste of shame and regret, because deep down I wasn't that bad, but sometimes (I justified myself) you have to be forceful to undo relationships that have no future.

I never heard from Elena again, I thought it was for the best and although I regretted it I did not call her so as not to awaken false hopes in her, I was depressed for many weeks, because the nobility of my subconscious accused me from the depths of my being. And I went back to being the usual loner, not having someone to share my life with in the way I would have liked, not having someone to talk to after leaving work, living with memories of my most beautiful moments that I enjoyed. with the two sisters.

# CHAPTER EIGHTH

I began to try to distract my mind by going to the gym every day, it was an incentive to entertain my mind with the routine and exhausting exercises, and sometimes I would chat quickly with one of the athletes, I always carried Dalila's photo in my wallet and one afternoon I I was talking to a woman who went to the gym at the same time, for some reason she asked me: have I seen him somewhere?... I think in a real estate office, is that true? Of course I did tell her, and trying to get a business card, I accidentally dropped my wallet and the cards and with them Dalila's photo were distributed on the floor, when I bent down to pick them up, she tried to help me and grabbed along with some cards the photo of my beloved.

With the curiosity of a woman, she looked at her, and told me: I think I know her, I felt like a flame running over my face, I felt tickles in my stomach and my legs were shaking, when she held out her hand to me with the few cards she had. I had picked up along with the photo of Delilah, I couldn't grab them because my hands were shaking, the surprised lady asked me what's wrong? I answered confused; I think it's the exercise, but tell me where do you know her from? And she told me, I think if I'm not mistaken I saw her in a store.

Trying to hide my anxiety to know more details, I invited her to drink a fruit juice with protein, so that she would have more time to tell me what she desperately wanted to know. Very excited, the lady began to tell me that she thought she had seen her in a supermarket. and that he thought it was her, but that she looked different without the uniform, but what seemed to him to be a detail that he couldn't forget were her beautiful green eyes. I almost fell over with excitement, and anxiously asked him for the name of the supermarket and the address.

The next morning I headed to the reference site, and for what I had thanked the lady who had been part of destiny that crossed my path. I had called in sick so I wasn't in a hurry, but when I got to the store I couldn't find anyone who wore any uniform and who looked anything like my beloved, so I went into the supermarket to ask the employees if they could give me some information, no one said anything so I parked in front hoping to see her at any moment. The day passed and he did not arrive, but since I knew by reference the color of the uniform, I presumed that it would be his day of rest, so I decided to arrive the next day. In any case, my illness could last up to five days since I had never called in sick.

The next day, very early in the morning, I went to the same place as the day before, with the hope of being able to locate her and finally put an end to the doubt that plagued me day after day, and that did not allow me to be happy or make anyone happy. Only two young women from a religious organization that collected donations to help the poor arrived, one of them had green eyes and black hair tied up with a kind of hat, but that was it, I timidly approached her and asked her if she knew Dalila showed him her photograph, she told me that she did not know her and that due to the ethics of the organization she could not give me any information. So I asked her for her phone number with the idea of making a donation, but she was suspicious and told me that if I wanted to make a donation, I could do it there with her, so depositing some money in the little jar she had with me, I left.

I didn't sit idly by, so I went home and started looking in the phone book for the names of religious organizations and their addresses, with the idea of going to the offices and waiting for the people who worked in them to arrive or leave. There weren't many of them who wore that type of uniform, so I went to set up a shift at the entrance of one of them and at the branch near the area, I was there until late at night, until the last of the people arrived. ; It did not arrive, and none of those who entered and who were men and women came out during the time I was there. The next morning I arrived very early and the same people who had entered came out again, so I went to another office of the organization that looked similar, but they had already left to their respective collection places and I had to take a tour of the nearby shopping centers while it was time to go wait for their return to the base.

And the miracle happened, it was her…. and she was just as pretty, she looked like a white dove in her uniform, she was the same as I remembered her, but despite my anxiety I didn't dare call her, I already knew where she was, and I would have time to find out what she had done. my life, everything shook, I felt that my heart was making the noise of a herd of runaway steeds and I felt a sensation of vertigo, I had to close my eyes and lie down on the back of the car seat, I felt that my legs were weakening and I didn't have the courage to drive for a long time, until I suddenly started the car and headed home. I had to thank my God for the opportunity to find it and at the same time acknowledge my old enemy (destiny) who now was vindicated with the opportunity to find my beloved, the woman of my dreams, the one who had been able to awaken true love in me, the only one who was capable of awakening my most beautiful feelings even in our most exquisite and overwhelming moments of pleasure.

I arrived home like a drunk, my euphoria was so great that I started screaming like a madman, I found her, I found her, yes, yes, ha, ha, ha, and I threw myself on the couch as if it were a stuffed toy, with hands and legs open and laughing like crazy, but suddenly I stopped laughing, I got serious and started thinking; I cannot celebrate yet, although it is true that I found her, that does not guarantee that she will be mine again, that does not guarantee that she will fill the house with joy and that she will agree to love me again and that we can be happy as I wanted, It could be that she had a romantic partner and that instead of being happy to see me, I only served as a hindrance to the fulfillment of her life.

I thought; God does not give two glories together, so I had to do a series of investigations before making my triumphant appearance, to be sure what to expect and to know what I had in my favor and what I had against, so I left my joy and I entered a stage of disappointment and uncertainty, which began to corrode my soul and give me more questions than answers. What will happen if she already has someone in her life? Well, in so long I don't think I've been able to resist loneliness, and what's more, what explanation could I give? If I asked why I was looking for her until now and what I had done with my life, the truth is that I had not been a saint and perhaps that is why I distrusted that she had also done the same, because the lion thinks that everyone is his condition.

What I had been wishing for for so long now seemed to me like it would have been better if it had not happened, all the illusion that I had maintained for so long now seemed to me to have been a waste of time, but in the depths of my soul a little light appeared. That he was telling me; don't rush to judgments and wait to see what you find out and then conclude, so I decided to take the whole week of illness, then I would try to explain to my boss how serious my illness was. And I began to arrive very early in the morning at the office and follow the vehicle in which they were traveling and keep an eye on the place where she was left to carry out her duties.

She was an Angel to convince donors to leave enough for the most needy people, with the sweetness of her face there was no one who could resist donating even a few coins, her operational partner would talk to her very occasionally like wanting to get her out of her self-absorption that was becoming more evident at times, and I think that deep down she was grateful, because despite her smile you could see the sadness in her soul, which caused a certain lack of spark in her beautiful eyes. I was watching her for three days from inside my car and putting on dark glasses and a sports cap that hid my appearance very well, so I looked at her without being seen. The truth is that it was an ordeal for me to have her so close and not be able to tell him; my love I came for you and you come back to me, or reach out and hug her and kiss her delicious lips that had kissed me in every way for so long.

During the three days I had been buying drinks and food for her and her friend or colleague, asking the cashier of the business to tell her that a client of the business had invited them, I wanted her not to suffer in any way while I was around her. her, but I began to feel that I was becoming more humanized from the moment I found her, because in my subconscious I thought: if for some reason she was already engaged, I would help her in some way to make her happy, since she deserved it as a reward for how much she had suffered because of the events and my foolish way of loving her, plus I had enough to share, since I had invested in a particular company, a technology company and luckily its shares had reached a high price, in addition to high annual percentage dividends.

Seven years had passed, she was now twenty-five and she was still just as beautiful and beautiful, but now a halo of maturity decorated her, it was clear that life's experiences had made her stronger and more intelligent, more analytical and distrustful, since she did not allow The men who donated approached her a lot and she always remained on the defensive, I liked her way and I thought that in that way it would be unlikely that someone would approach her and could have convinced her. At least that was my hope, it was Friday and I didn't know if she would show up for work on Saturday, so I was attentive when she entered the establishment to buy something to drink and that of course I had left paid for, so at that time At that moment I approached her companion and asked her if they would come the next day since I had forgotten my wallet and wanted to donate some money. She answered that they dedicated Saturday to prayer and reading their holy book, so I thought that It would be until Monday when I would surely clear up my doubts when facing the love of my life.

Saturday will beíFor me it was the same as any other Saturday in the last seven after the breakup with Elena,

I wish she was having a good time because she deserved better than a nerd like me, she was young and pretty, as well as beautiful and elegant, also intelligent and very good lover, so I thought she deserved a good partner for her life. Sometimes I don't understand people, because around nine in the morning, the time when I'm usually making my coffee and getting ready to read the newspaper, I heard a knock on the door and, in my pajamas as I was, I prepared to open it. My surprise was greater because it was Elena who was playing. She gave me a smile with a gesture of uncertainty and submissively told me: I brought you something for breakfast. Can I come in? I felt moved as well as grateful, because despite my poor performance The previous time, he was demonstrating his human qualities and did not harbor any resentment.

Come in, I told her, and serving coffee I invited her to eat together, she sat down very happily, her attitude had changed as she felt well received and when we were about to start eating very slowly she told me: forgive me for my attitude the other night, no. I know how I could behave that way, I think I was hysterical because of some personal problems, but I ask you to forgive me and forget, will you? Of course I forgave her, although I had nothing to say to her because the one who had done things wrong had It was me, however I told her that I also apologized if I had hurt her physically or morally in any way, and she said again: of course everything is forgotten, a clean slate. I couldn't give him false hope so I told him that we had to talk, but that we should eat first and then talk, I didn't want to spoil his food by giving him bad news.

So after finishing the food I asked him to sit down since I had to tell him something; She sat down and raised her little ears as if she were a bunny paying close attention. I sat on the sofa next to her, but trying to keep a safe distance so as not to fall into temptation, however, little by little she approached me and, taking one of my hands, she placed it on one of her enormous, solid breasts. I instinctively walked away from her, so she insisted and told me: I think your forgiveness was not true because you are walking away from me as if you were angry, right?

I couldn't start the game again, so I asked her to let me continue, she told me: I'm listening to you but don't take your hand away from me, so thinking there was nothing wrong, I continued; Look, our relationship can't be, you have a lot of life ahead of you for you to meet the true love of your life and don't insist on a relationship that won't take us anywhere, plus I'm dating another woman (I lied) but She very confidently answered me: I know it's a lie because I've been spying on you and I know it's not true, although I don't know what you're looking for in the parking lot of that store, but you haven't met anyone. Why do you insist on lie?

I didn't know what to say and when I wanted to react it was too late, my body did not ask for explanations and having been without a woman as a complement, he took advantage of the beautiful female he had and I fell for her charms and the mischief she had to seduce me, and we fell into a vibrant and passionate trance of sex and madness that took us to the most remote places in time and space. It was a night in which I gave her my most delicate style of loving, it was where I made her feel happy and enjoy the most pleasant and sublime orgasms, it was when she actually felt loved but she also sensed it was the farewell to something she had. a happy ending.

We were exhausted and suffocated, but with satisfaction on the surface and wanting the night not to end so we could continue loving each other, to continue transporting ourselves to that place where there is only room for two. And we continued throughout the night until the dawn of twilight told us that it would be better if we rested to be able to survive so much waste of energy. We woke up around ten in the morning and when I saw her there in my bed, naked and so beautiful, so defenseless and so provocative, when I felt the smoothness of her body and the solidity of her curves and her large breasts, which seemed volcanoes pointing towards the sky, waiting to find the caress of my lips that when it landed on them ignited my instincts and I possessed her again, I couldn't help it even though I felt guilty for being unfaithful to her now that I had found her, what a dilemma!

However, after I no longer had the strength left for anything, I made the decision to ask her to wait a month to define my feelings, because even though I loved Dalila so much, I couldn't stop succumbing to Elena's charms, and she She agreed and promised me that she would respect my decision although she knew that she was going to die if I left her, because it would be almost impossible to find someone who could love her the way I loved her, so at sunset she left, with the promise of waiting for a month and at the end of which he was waiting for my call to ask him to come and give me all his love.

I knew that all the women who were with me after Dalila's departure had only motivated sexual desire in me, but that was the reason they did not leave a mark like my beloved had done, who even after seven years and more was still in love. of her, and more than wanting her I hoped to find her to continue loving her, I knew that she was the only woman who awakened in me the desire to love and not just the need for sex, that's why I wanted to know to what extent she had been able to remain chaste and not giving her love to another man, that was the mystery that kept my soul in suspense and what had made me ask Elena for a deadline, deep down my most fervent desire was to know that she still loved me and that she would give me the opportunity to be happy for the rest of our days.

I know that I had not been a correct man, I know that my weakness had always been to pursue my satisfaction without caring if they loved me or not, but now it was different, I had finally realized that love is a very important part of the union. of two people, that the basic thing will always be to put love before any other sense, and that if I wanted that relationship to last, it would be essential that that relationship be based on love, the greatest of human feelings, and why not until of the irrational animals that look for their partner to love them in their own way and provide them with the care they need, and try to give them their share of sex but as a complement and to keep the flame of love lit.

Maybe it would seem very cheesy, but in reality Delilah had taught me the path of love, she had been able to sacrifice herself by leaving my side and going through who knows what vicissitudes, in exchange for our love lasting in the distance before it was transformed. in hatred, resentment, or any other feeling motivated by my unhealthy jealousy, which believed I saw everywhere what did not exist anywhere, except in my deranged mind that had been able to transform my love for her into something very different and abhorrent, something that had us in the situation we were in now.

But now that I had found her, I hoped that it would be a reason for reconciliation and to be able to start from scratch, to awaken our feelings that had fallen asleep in a certain way, but that at least had kept me in constant restlessness during the seven years and more, and that they had helped me learn the lesson and appreciate the greatness of their love. I only asked heaven that now that I was a few hours away from our meeting, an unforeseen event would not occur that would ruin my hopes, now I was begging merciless destiny to please continue with its truce and give me the opportunity to to finally be completely happy.

Monday was approaching, the most anticipated day for me, I knew that my happiness was at stake, the happiness of Delilah and that of those who were related in some way to us, because I had plans that only she could tell, only her. I could tell him all the illusions that my mind and soul harbored and that I could not tell anyone else. It was my secret and it would stop being so the moment Dalila deigned to listen to me and return to my side, to love her and share with me everything she had achieved motivated by her love.

I wanted to sleep to have strength for the next day, but I could only toss and turn in bed, my head was a pile of hopes and dreams that I hoped would come true, I made plans of what I would say when I saw her, but I thought that in the end After all, spontaneous is the most sincere thing that can be expressed, so I would let what I was feeling come out into my mouth at the moment I saw her pretty face and the flame of happiness in her eyes.

I think I managed to fall asleep well into the night, but I still had a dream with shocks and in my subconscious I was afraid that she would tell me that my search had been in vain and that I might as well keep my dreams, that she had my own and I would forget everything. I woke up sweating from so much tension and confusion of thoughts and I went to the bathroom to wet my face and try to relax, be positive and not lose faith, so after another few minutes that seemed like hours I fell asleep again.

I woke up all sleepy, so I had to drink two cups of coffee to wake up well so I could go to work, it was necessary for my boss to know that I had not died and to work hard to make up for the time I was absent, my boss was He was happy to see me and I had to invent a white lie, and at the same time ask permission to leave an hour early, I wanted to arrive on time for the appointment I had scheduled and I didn't want to waste a single minute of what I hoped would be something unforgettable.

It was somewhat stressful to wait for seven hours, but then I realized that seven hours are nothing compared to seven years and more, so I gathered my courage and waited patiently until my watch told me that it was time to go to the expected meeting. My legs were shaking and I felt like a teenager on his first date. I couldn't find the words to open my conversation, but the important thing was to arrive and face the very difficult situation. After parking my car, I kept observing where she was located, to suddenly appear in front of her to see what her first reaction was, I entered through the door at the opposite end, so that when I came out where she was she saw me immediately, but it was like this Well, when I was dealing with a person to request a donation, he didn't realize that I was leaving.

Suddenly I was standing in front of her, and she did not notice my presence until she stopped talking to said person. When she saw me standing in front of her, she was surprised and opened her eyes wide. She could not speak a word until I called her name. Hello Delilah. André... managed to say very weakly and the colleague who had followed the entire course of events, surprised, told me: that's not his name, please don't bother. I ignored his words and restarting the conversation I told him: we have to talk, please come with me for a moment and then if you want you can continue with your task.

Instinctively he approached his partner and pleadingly told me: please don't do anything to me that wasn't my fault. The classmate energetically told me: if you don't leave I will call the police, so you better leave. Very respectfully I told him: Miss, this is none of your business, and I just want to talk to my wife and I don't mean any harm to her, Delilah please allow me just a few minutes, we will talk like civilized people and then I will leave, I promise.

Very timid, she accepted, but not before saying something to the other woman, she probably asked her to be attentive in case something happened to her, there were some tables in the corridor of the store and I asked her to sit down, I couldn't stop looking at her beautiful face. , her beautiful big eyes that radiated all the beauty of her soul, and even after so long I felt that they also radiated love and a little fear, I asked her to calm down because the reason for being there in front of her was nothing more than to break the ice from a distance of more than seven years, and that at the end of a long search I had finally had the opportunity to find it, and that I would now do everything in my power not to lose it again.

He stared at me and asked me: Don't you think it's a little late for that? I hastened to answer; of course not, you have taught me to love, to feel loved, to feel infected with the beauty of your soul, to realize that my love is only yours and that no woman will be able to take it away from you, because I come to offer it to you and promise you that I am a different man and that I will try to be even better, so I ask you to return to my side, but if you already have another love, even if I suffer for the rest of my life, I promise that I will not be a hindrance in your life .

He looked at me intently as if he wanted to weigh the words I had said to him, as if he wanted to analyze me to see if I was telling the truth, to see through my eyes if what I said came directly from the heart and he said to me: do you really not hold a grudge against me? ?, not really, time made me understand that I was acting wrongly, that my behavior was not appropriate for a person who loves the way I love you, that is why time taught me to love you without conditioning. no nature, to understand that if you tell me that you don't love me it is because I was to blame for your decision, but also to understand that no matter what you tell me, my love for you will always be the same, so I want your answer.

I don't know what to say, I know it sounds strange but I have a commitment to humanity and if I return to you I will no longer have the opportunity to continue doing so, maybe you don't understand me but after so many years I think my love for you became more a very nice memory, and perhaps you have clung to a memory and your determination to correct what you did, so it seems to me that the best thing would be for us to give ourselves a deadline and see if our feelings can get back on track or if Otherwise that doesn't work, it's because everything came to an end.

I knew it wasn't going to be easy, so I had to accept his proposal, but I asked him to give me the opportunity to show him that I was a different man, to come to my house that was also his house and to realize what had achieved, to offer him a different life. It was then that he told me, I know we won't be able to have a home like we dreamed of and you know why, a home without children is like a garden without flowers, don't you think? Without stopping to see his beautiful green eyes I told him: that you do good in the name of God, and that your fear is that you will no longer be able to help people, but don't you think that there are other ways to do his will?, for example: adopting children who have been orphaned and that they need the warmth of a home and the affection of parents, that although they do not know that they are not the real ones, they will love them just as if they were their own, don't you think that that is doing the will of God, loving others? How does he love us?

She had no argument, she remained thoughtful and told me: you know, when I left home I didn't know where to go, I had no clothes or money, only the faith of finding a place where I could live and start my life, fortunately I found to these people who have given me their help and the opportunity to get closer to God, trying to be better every day and do good selflessly, so after we look at each other as friends and if our relationship grows, then I will ask you to talk to the director of the organization I am in to thank in this way for the opportunity they gave me and to see where destiny takes us.

It seemed like just what he asked of me, so I agreed and asked him to see each other every afternoon, even if it was just for a few minutes, and that on Sunday we would go to eat somewhere and if he was suspicious, we would go with his partner as a guest. You know, you are still just as beautiful and beautiful, just as you have always been in my mind, just as I dreamed of you even when I was awake. Without even thinking about it, I asked him, do you want to marry me? For the three laws, for the civil, for the church and because I love you.

He shuddered and I don't know what feeling appeared on his face and after a few seconds of uncertainty he told me: Really? Aren't you kidding? You know that would make me immensely happy, knowing that our love is blessed by God, and without saying anything he approached me to place a tender kiss on my mouth, I felt as if the petals of a rose were caressing my lips. , as if a tender butterfly caressed me with its wings, and I felt a warmth run through my face, it seemed as if it had injected me with an elixir that motivated my body and that inexplicably my heart began to beat rapidly, to feel that it was the potion of its lips that gave reason to my existence and I felt like the happiest man on earth.

I left with the illusion of a boyfriend in love, with the arrow of Eros (Cupid) in my heart, but I knew that I would not die from that wound. That same afternoon, when I arrived home overjoyed, I called Elena, I told her that I really had no interest in our relationship and that it would be best for her to continue on her way and that the right man for her would arrive at the right time, neither before or after, that I appreciated all his attention but that ours could not be, he cried for a few minutes, but after time he told me: I know that you love another and I cannot compete with her, but I wish you the best and that be happy and saying goodbye cut off.

# EPILOGUE

It wasn't just one week that we saw each other, it was two in which we seemed like lovebirds in love, we were satisfied to have a little romance to revive our feelings that were like in a coma, we felt happy to hold hands and talk about so many things. ways to help humanity, and how nice it would be to have a real home full of love and a couple of children who would bring joy to our lives and accompany us in our old age. I had gone to thank the director of the institution and bring him a check with a considerable amount of donation, and at the same time to invite him to our civil and religious wedding on a certain date, I did not want to break the charm, so I asked him to be in the institution until the day of the religious marriage, so we had to wait until the designated day.

It was a simple wedding, in which only a few of her companions and some of my closest friends arrived, and after the celebration that was at home, we headed to our honeymoon in the beautiful and old city of San Francisco, where We gave free rein to all the love that united us and continued to unite us. It was an unforgettable honeymoon, in which we rekindled the fire of our love and where we made plans so that our lives would receive in payment for our sufferings, all the love of us and those who would be part of our lives. I had finally learned to love and stop being just the sex machine, I had finally put everything in its place, to understand that love is everything and that sex is only a complement.

After a few months, in which a good lawyer had obtained Dalila's documents, we went to Mexico to visit the beautiful places we had known on our odyssey. After our return we went to meet our future children, a beautiful three-year-old girl. years (Diana) and little André who was four, so we were already a beautiful family, and where we were immensely happy and forged the lives of our heirs that fill us with pride and satisfaction. Three years later, we had received invitations from Rosaura's children who had graduated as Lawyers, and in the invitation there was a thank you to their sponsor and friend André, it was a fair reward for my selfless contribution, but one that had borne fruit.

# FIN